Cake Pop
Crush

Suzanne Nelson

SCHOLASTIC INC.

For Aunt Carol and Grandma Sue,
two resilient women I admire and love

Copyright © 2013 by Suzanne Nelson

All rights reserved. Published by Scholastic Inc., *Publishers since
1920.* SCHOLASTIC and associated logos are trademarks and/or
registered trademarks of Scholastic Inc.

The publisher does not have any control over and does not
assume any responsibility for author or third-party websites
or their content.

This book is a work of fiction. Names, characters, places, and
incidents are either the product of the author's imagination or
are used fictitiously, and any resemblance to actual persons,
living or dead, business establishments, events, or locales is
entirely coincidental.

ISBN 978-0-545-85734-5

10 9 8 7 6   17 18 19 20

Printed in the U.S.A.   40
First printing 2016

Book design by Jennifer Rinaldi Windau

Chapter One

I knew I shouldn't be awake. My eyes opened onto a gleaming moon and stars outside my window, and I had that topsy-turvy feeling of being out of sync with time. The clock said 4:30 A.M. I shut my eyes and tucked deeper into my covers, but it was no use. My stomach pinched uncomfortably. School was starting again after the two-week winter break, and my nerves knew it.

There was only one cure for that: baking.

In my pajamas, I tiptoed out of my bedroom and down the shadowy hallway. My dad had left half an hour ago to go to work at our family bakery, Say It With Flour. So I knew he wouldn't be hovering over me with his running commentary: "Alicia, you're sifting the flour too quickly," or "Don't beat the eggs to death." My five-year-old brother, Roberto, was still sleeping, and I could hear Abuelita Rosa snoring happily (and loudly) away in her bedroom. So I had the kitchen all to myself.

I carefully laid out all of my measuring cups and spoons on the counter, then got my mixing bowls ready. Everything had to be in place before I could start so there'd be no missed steps or surprises. Surprise is the easiest way to ruin perfect baking. Open an oven door too soon, and the cake falls. Drop a cold egg into hot butter and it curdles. I've never liked surprises.

When I was satisfied that I had everything ready, I turned on the oven. None of my friends could ever get away with using stove tops and ovens alone, but I'd been baking with my parents since before I could walk, so my dad had given me free reign in our kitchen long ago.

My abuelita loves to tell the story of how, when I was a newborn, I had colic. Apparently that means I cried for hours at a time for no reason at all. Go figure. My mom even made this sling for me so that she could hold me close while she baked. I still cried constantly, until the morning Mom put a small shaker of cinnamon in my hand. She was baking *capirotada*, a kind of Mexican bread pudding. She'd been trying to get the recipe right for weeks, but it wasn't working. I started shaking that cinnamon like a rattle, and pretty soon I'd sprinkled it all over the bread. Abuelita said I fell asleep in that sling clutching the cinnamon in my tiny little fist, and my mom's *capirotada* finally came out perfect, all because of me. Every day after that, my mom gave me a spice to hold while she baked, and Abuelita swears that I always knew when to add just the right dash to every treat. Maybe that was the start of it all, or maybe it was just a story Abuelita had made up. It didn't really matter. Because like other kids were born for math or art or sports, I was born to bake. To me, there is nothing better in the world than a hot oven and a spice rack full of possibilities.

I grabbed my tattered recipe book, flipped on the small TV on our kitchen counter, and scrolled through the DVR listings until I came to my favorite show, *The Baking Guru*. I pushed PLAY, then smiled as Renata DeLuca's exotically beautiful face flashed onto the screen. I DVR her show every day on the Food Network, and I keep a running log of her recipes in my notebook.

Renata's claim to fame is a chocolate buttermilk cake with ginger icing topped with almond shavings. It has a secret ingredient, too, and it's the only recipe she won't share on her show. Legend has it that she made the cake for the president once, and afterward he placed enough orders for that cake to last his entire lifetime. Did I believe it? Yes, I did. Because every single Renata DeLuca recipe I'd ever made was amazing.

"Welcome, fellow bakers!" she said now. "I hope you're all enjoying a bright, sunshiny day!"

"Not yet." I glanced out the window at the still-dark sky.

"Well, even if it's not sunny where you are, it will be after we make our Lemon Sunrise cake pops!"

She ticked off all the ingredients, and I started collecting them from the fridge and pantry.

She flipped her long waves of curls over her shoulder and once again I wished that I could get my thick, stick-straight mane of chocolaty hair to curl as perfectly as hers. My mom had curly hair, too, and in some strange way, watching Renata always makes me feel a little closer to my mom again. She died when I was nine, and the memories I had of her used to be so sharp that sometimes, for a split second, I would forget she was gone. But lately, some of those memories have gotten cloudier, harder to call up when I want them. But I do remember her hair always smelled like chocolate, with just the tiniest hint of roses.

As I laid out my ingredients, I thought about school. Sure, I was excited to see my friends again. But I hated the idea of the unknown assignments and tests lying in wait for me. Once I had them all plotted out on my calendar, I could make a plan for studying. Right now, though, all those unknowns were ballooning in my mind.

But as I listened to Renata's cheery voice, I forgot about the unknowns. I forgot about everything except the steady weight of the measuring cups in my hands. The second my hands dipped into the bag of pillowy flour, my stomach untied itself, and by the time Roberto stumbled bleary-eyed into the kitchen asking what smelled so good, I was ready to face my first day back at Oak Canyon Middle School.

When I stepped onto the outdoor quad with my box of two dozen Lemon Sunrise cake pops, most of the kids were still standing around in the sunshine, catching up with friends and gossip. No one seemed to want to move toward the lockers or classrooms yet. I spotted my best friends, Gwen and Tansy, near the open-air amphitheater, waving me over with grins.

"Ali!" Tansy grabbed me in a hug. "I missed you!" Tansy is always quick with hugs, and she smiles so much that sometimes *my* mouth actually hurts. Even the tight black curls that frame her face bounce along happily when she moves.

I laughed. "Tansy, you just saw me at the movies three days ago."

Tansy shrugged, giving a little giggle. "I know, but not at *school.*"

Meanwhile, Gwen honed in on the box I was holding. "Is that what I think it is?" she asked, twirling her slender side braid. The rest of Gwen's hair is honey-colored, but she'd used lemon juice and good ol' California sunshine to lighten the braid to a golden blond. Then — in classic Gwen fashion — she'd woven tiny fuchsia feathers into the strand.

I nodded, smiling. Over our years of friendship, Tansy and Gwen have developed uncanny cake-pop radar. "A welcome-back present."

"Just what I needed," Gwen said with a grin. "Reinforcements. First day back is such a killer."

"You know what I always say . . ." Before I could finish the sentence, Gwen and Tansy did it for me.

"There is no crisis a cake pop can't solve," they said in unison, then broke into giggles.

"We've only heard it a million times," Gwen said. She tried to grab the box from me.

"Watch it, chica," I teased. "I don't *have* to share."

"Okay, okay, I'm sorry," Gwen said, raising her hands in surrender. "You know I'm a slave to your baking. You just have to keep your cheesiness in check sometimes."

"It's not cheesy," I said, smiling. "It's one of life's great truths."

I opened the box, revealing the pops I had stuck neatly into foam in the center. Two dozen pale yellow suns topped with dainty marshmallow daisies.

"Isn't it kind of early to be eating cake?" Tansy asked hesitantly.

"Hey, cake pops are part of a balanced, nutritious breakfast," Gwen said. "Didn't you get the memo?"

Tansy picked one up and spun it between her fingers. "Oh, Ali, I can't," she said. "It's too pretty to eat."

"Nope," I said. "You two are my official taste testers. You can't get out of it." I leaned toward her. "Go on, try it. Bite that daisy's head right off. You know you want to."

"No problem here," Gwen said, biting the whole top off the pop at once. She grinned around chipmunk cheeks. "Mmmm. Absolute ambrosia. Really."

Tansy looked uncertainly at the cake pop, then took a gentle bite. She closed her eyes. "Yummers," she said. "What is it?"

"Lemon poppy seed with cream cheese icing." Even if I made a tofu and pâté pop, Tansy would probably say it was delish. She was just that eager to please. But Gwen was my truth teller. And that she was already reaching for seconds . . . well, that said something.

"How did you come up with that brill' combo?" Gwen asked between bites.

"I didn't," I said somewhat sheepishly. "Renata DeLuca made them on her show."

"Ah, Renata, goddess of baking, we salute you." Gwen bent in an exaggerated curtsy toward an imaginary Renata, and nearly knocked into Harris Clark.

"Whoa, Gwen." Harris laughed, showing off his bright smile. "I know I can kick a mean winning goal, but you don't have to bow, really."

"Don't worry, it wasn't for your benefit," Gwen said, playing it cool, but her cheeks blushed raspberry.

Harris turned his adorable brown eyes in my direction. "Hey, Ali. I came over to see if you had any of your awesome cake pops to spare. The guys could use some extra energy for practice later."

Now it was my turn to blush. "Um, sure," I said, fumbling with the box lid. "Help yourself."

As Harris grabbed a handful of cake pops, I glanced at Tansy and Gwen, who were both wide-eyed, their mouths two little donut holes. Harris was the star of the Oak Canyon soccer team, and one of the most popular boys in our grade. But he was also the kind of kid who ignored the rules of the school social ladder. He was friendly with everybody, and because of that, everybody liked him, too. Of course, most of the time when he came our direction, it was in search of food. But I didn't mind. Any time Harris bothered to talk to the three of us, it took hours for our pulses to return to normal.

"Thanks, Ali," he said, then bit into a pop. "Wow. That's really good. I can't believe you just give these away. You should sell them!"

I smiled, my heart thrumming happily. "Thanks. I'm working on it."

"Well, see you guys later." He waved at Tansy and tugged on Gwen's side braid.

"Hey!" Gwen snatched back her braid protectively, but she was smiling. "Don't mess with the Gwenliness."

Harris laughed as he walked off to rejoin his soccer buddies. They all made mad grabs for the cake pops, then waved their thanks in my direction while I beamed.

"He's such a nice guy," Tansy whispered.

"He's such a cutie," I added.

"He is such a sucker for anything edible," Gwen quipped. "Boys . . . they're human garbage disposals." But she smiled as she rolled her eyes.

I was about to rally the girls to head for our lockers when I caught sight of a sleek black limo easing to a stop in the school parking lot.

"Hey," I said, nudging them, "what is *that* all about?"

"Hmmmm," Gwen said, her eyes narrowing. "Maybe Sarah forgot her backpack at the royal palace and Daddy brought it for her."

Sarah Chan was the mayor's only daughter and the only girl in the school who had a house so big it was called "Chan Manor." No joke. Last year, Sarah had single-handedly driven half of the seventh-grade girls into an all-white wardrobe trend that had lasted months. Then, when she'd gotten tired of the lack of color, she had started wearing crimson orchids tucked behind her ears. And guess what? Days later, when Sarah walked through the school hallways, a Red Sea of orchid-wearing mimics parted before her.

"I don't think so," Tansy whispered, nodding toward where Sarah was sitting with her friends. Their table was under the only tree in the entire quad — the coolest, shadiest spot here. Even in January, Southern California could hit the mid-70s, so shade was always a plus. And on the blistering hot days of early fall and late spring, Sarah's was the table everyone wanted but couldn't have. "Look," Tansy added. "She's staring, too."

Sure enough, Sarah's perfect crescent eyebrows were arched in surprise, and she had her hand cupped over her mouth, whispering to Lissie and Jane. The three of them made up the great triumvirate at Oak Canyon. I didn't totally dislike Sarah. Actually, embarrassing as it was to admit, I was a little in awe of her. Still, it was fun to see her caught off guard by the limo, too.

We all watched as Principal Dalton came striding out of the school, followed closely by Vice Principal Wilton and Mrs. Hughes, the school secretary.

"Wow," Gwen muttered. "A red-carpet welcome by Oak Canyon standards. I can practically see Dalton sweating from here."

"Maybe it's a celebrity!" Tansy said in a hushed squeal. Tansy always dreamed big. She was the optimist of our group. "We could have a movie star attending our school."

"Um, Tansy, we live in Oak Canyon, not Beverly Hills." Gwen gave Tansy a good-natured eye roll. "We're too far off the 405 for celebs."

The limo door opened, and a middle-aged man in a suit stepped into the sunshine with a cell phone pressed to his ear. The man shook hands with the school staff, but he did it quickly and absently, all the while chatting into his phone. He glanced back at the open car door a few times, and then, frowning, snapped his phone shut and stuck his head back into the car. A full minute went by before he finally straightened and stepped out of the way to let a boy our age climb out. The boy's cargo pants and faded blue T-shirt looked out of place next to the man's suit. There was a scowl on his lips, and his face was half hidden by blond waves of thick hair.

"Not a celeb," Gwen confirmed.

"But cute enough to be one," Tansy whispered with a grin.

It was true. Even from across the quad, I could see the boy was tall, with creamy olive skin. Definitely cute. *Very.*

Principal Dalton extended his hand to the boy, but the boy simply grabbed the class schedule that Mrs. Hughes was holding out to him. Then he brushed past the welcoming committee, heading toward the lockers.

"Cute with a serious attitude," I said. I watched him until he disappeared around the corner of the gymnasium. The man in the suit was already getting back into the limo, cell phone stuck to his ear again. "And if that's his dad, then the problem must be genetic." Still, though, I thought I'd seen a hint of something else on the boy's face besides anger. Had it been the tiniest bit of sadness?

"Maybe he's just having a bad day," Tansy tried. "It happens."

"How anyone who rides to school in a limo could have a bad day is beyond me," Gwen said.

The bell rang, and the mass of kids in the quad gave an audible groan. But soon enough everyone broke into chaos, shouldering backpacks and drifting down the outdoor hallways. Gwen, Tansy, and I hurried to our lockers, and then to our classes.

I was sure my case of nerves from this morning was under control, but that was until I walked into my first-period science class.

Because sitting at the desk next to mine, the desk that had been empty all year until today, was the blond-haired mystery boy. With his arms folded tightly across his chest and his chin tucked into the collar of his shirt, he looked completely miserable.

I dropped into my seat as Mr. Jenkins called the class to order.

"Ladies and gentlemen," he said. "We have a new student this semester." He nodded toward my neighbor. "This is Dane McGuire. He just moved here from New Orleans. I know you'll help give him a warm welcome to our school."

A few guys muttered noncommittal "Hey's" or raised hands in greeting, while most of the girls offered much less subtle doe-eyes and smiles.

"Hi," Dane mumbled. He gave one nod of acknowledgement, then resumed staring at his desk with great intensity.

"All right," Mr. Jenkins continued. "Today we'll be starting a new unit on marine biology. Next week is our whale-watching field trip to Long Beach, and we have a lot of material to cover beforehand."

Mr. Jenkins droned on, and as I scribbled meticulous notes for color coding later (my fail-safe study technique), Dane pulled his chin deeper into his collar. Scowling was the only contribution he made to class for the rest of the period. And when class ended, he left, taking his frown with him.

By the time lunch rolled around, I'd found my routine again. I was filling my calendar with assignment due dates and scheduled exams. The unknowns that had loomed over me this morning were shrinking, and I was able to enjoy my turkey sandwich beside Gwen and Tansy in the sunshiny quad.

But the new boy, Dane, didn't look like he was enjoying anything. He had chosen an isolated spot in the corner of the quad near one of the trash cans for his eating post.

"Hey." I elbowed Gwen, watching. "Sarah's about to make a move."

Sarah Chan loped toward Dane, fluttering her lashes. She motioned for him to join her in her shady spot, but he shook his head, his expression never changing. Sarah shrugged good-naturedly as she walked away, but her smile looked a smidge forced now.

"Check out Mr. Attitude," I said.

Gwen nodded. "Too good to eat with the commoners *or* the royals."

"Maybe not too good," Tansy said. "Maybe just not ready." Her face lit up. "Hey, Ali, why don't you give him one of your cake pops? I bet that would make his day."

I shook my head, glancing down at the box of pops I'd brought to lunch. "I can't just go up to him and give him one. Totally awkward." My cheeks cooked at the thought.

The lunch bell rang, and I sighed, thinking I'd gotten off the hook. I was wrong. As we were walking toward our lockers, Gwen spotted Dane at his. He was launching books into it, making sure every one made a loud bang.

"Here's the plan," Gwen whispered. "Leave him one anony-mously. Stick it in his locker with a note."

"No." I shook my head violently, but then Dane slammed his locker shut and walked away. Gwen and Tansy instantly had me by the arms, one pulling me, one pushing me toward his locker. Before I knew what was happening, Gwen grabbed a cake pop out of my pastry box and stuck it firmly into one of the locker vents. Much to my horror, it lodged there, safe and secure. I was about to yank it out, but something stopped me. Maybe Tansy was right. Maybe Dane needed a sign of friendship, something that said his new school wasn't so bad, after all. So, before I could stop myself, I quickly scribbled Welcome to Oak Canyon! on a slip of paper and wedged it into the vent next to the cake pop.

Giggling, my friends and I ran to our lockers. We grabbed our books quickly, and Tansy hurried off to math while Gwen and I walked toward the language arts building. Gwen had Spanish this period and I had English lit.

"So," Gwen asked as we reached the door to Mrs. Brach's English class, "are you going to show the Lemon Sunrise pops to your dad?"

I shrugged. "What's the point? He won't let me use them. He never does."

"It's worth a try," Gwen said. "I'll come with you to talk to him if you want, after school."

I laughed. "Gwennie, you *always* come with me after school." Gwen's parents both work in downtown LA, and they usually don't make it home until after dark. Gwen is pretty much a permanent fixture in my family. But my dad says sometimes children need extra family like they need extra toothbrushes, whatever that means. So Gwen hangs out with us almost every afternoon, which is more than fine by me.

She grinned impishly. "Hey, I'm trying to come up with a legit reason. Other than leeching snacks off your dad. Play along, please."

I latched on to her arm, giving her an exaggerated hug. "Yes, oh please come with me. I desperately need your help. *Please.*"

She nodded, giving a victorious smile. "Thanks. It's always nice to be appreciated."

I laughed. "I'll meet you at your locker after seventh."

The rest of the afternoon passed in a blur of new projects and assignments, and then, finally, the first day of the new semester was over. I beat Gwen to the lockers, and while I was slipping my homework into my book bag, I glanced up to see Dane pluck-ing my cake pop from his locker. I blushed, suddenly feeling completely ridiculous for putting it there in the first place. He held up the cake pop, inspecting it, then read the note.

I waited for a smile to break across his face. But it never came. He spun on his heel, walked right past me, and tossed the cake pop into the hall trash can. He hadn't even taken a single bite.

My face went from bake to broil, and suddenly I knew it was going to be impossible for me to become friends with Dane McGuire. Because sometimes, no matter how hard you try, all the sugar in the world can't sweeten up something gone sour.

Chapter Two

"I cannot *believe* he threw it away," Gwen said as we walked from school down Valencia Avenue. From the second I'd told her about the untimely death of my cake pop, Gwen hadn't been able to talk about anything else. She was taking it way more personally than I was.

"Maybe he's allergic to lemons," I tried. "Or maybe he thought someone was playing a joke on him?"

"Or maybe he's just a jerk," Gwen said with finality. "Which is too bad, because he was off to such a good start with that gorgeous face of his."

I shrugged, trying to pretend that it wasn't a big deal. But the fact was, it *was* insulting. I mean, who turns down cake? Seriously. "I'd rather forget about the whole thing," I said.

Suddenly, my cell phone chimed and so did Gwen's. We exchanged questioning glances, then checked our phones. We each had identical e-vites in our inboxes.

In flourishing script bordered by pink hearts and roses, the invitation read:

You are cordially invited to
Sarah Chan's Valentine's Birthday Soiree.
Saturday, February 16 at 3 P.M.
To be held in the backyard of Chan Manor.
Food will be served and the pool will be heated.
Bring your suits. And don't forget, in the spirit of
Valentine's Day, please wear red or pink!
See you all there!

"A soiree?" I snorted. "How did we even snag an invite, anyway? Sarah barely talks to us." Then I got my answer. I checked the guest list and gasped. "Gwen, she's invited the *entire* school."

"Of course she did." Gwen rolled her eyes. "Her backyard has its own zip code. It'll be the most expensive party of the year." She batted her eyes and curtsied. "Oh, whatever shall we wear to the ball, Princess Ali?" she said in a fake British accent.

"Surely not these peasant rags," I responded, motioning to our clothes.

We both cracked up, and kept up our accents for the rest of the walk. But the second we stepped through the back door of Say It With Flour, I stopped laughing. Something was wrong. Normally, our kitchen was filled with the sugary scent of cookies baking. There was nothing in the world better than that smell. But today, the kitchen's smell was off — a mixture of burnt toast and dishwashing liquid. And sure enough, when I looked in the sink, there were two scorched baking sheets soaking in sudsy water. I frowned at the mess, washed my hands, and grabbed my apron. Then I headed through the swinging doors into the main room with Gwen to find out what had happened.

Say It With Flour was the kind of place that people wanted to linger in. There was a quote from *Don Quixote* painted on the yellow wall behind the counter. It read, "With bread all sorrows are less." That, plus the round tables, teal-colored booths, and ceiling strung with colorful tin lanterns, set the cheerful mood.

We had a small but steady stream of regulars, and many of them had known my father since he opened the bakery with my mother just before I was born. Some stopped in the morning and ended up staying for hours. To them, my father wasn't just the shop owner; he was a friend.

I waved to Mr. Salez and Mr. Johnson, who were in their booth playing chess and munching on cookies.

"Hello, Alicia," they said in unison without breaking their concentration.

Mrs. Kerny, the ninety-something widow who came in every day to share a *cochinito* with her Chihuahua, waved to me over her cup of tea.

Finally, I arrived at the corner booth, where Abuelita Rosa and Roberto were hunkered down over Roberto's coloring book.

"Hola, niñitas." My grandmother pulled Gwen and me into a soft hug, and I breathed in the doughy smell of yeast and sugar on her apron. There was a fine dusting of flour in the bun at the nape of her neck.

"Daddy's down in the grumps," Roberto said, mixing up words like he always did.

"Is he?" I grinned and ruffled Roberto's hair.

Abuelita nodded. "He burned a whole batch of cookies already."

"That was Dad? Wow." When my dad started burning stuff, it was serious. "What happened?"

She clucked her tongue, shaking her head. "You need to ask *him*."

In the front of the shop, my dad stood staring out the huge bay window, his face pinched and pale. I started toward him, admiring our window display. It was full of golden Mexican sweet breads, all nestled cozily together — corn-shaped *elotitos* with their yummy custard filling, flaky and puffed-up *orejas* with their funny ear shape, the jelly-filled *pan fino* loaves with their delicate ridges and cinnamony goodness.

And front and center, just like always, were *conchas*, with their beautiful pink and yellow swirling crusts. They're baked with lots of butter, eggs, and sugar for sweetness and are made to look like giant seashells. *Conchas* were my mother's absolute favorite. My dad told me that my mom used to eat three *conchas* a day when she was pregnant with me. So every day, my dad bakes a fresh batch of *conchas* and puts three in the front window, like a little bit of baked love, just for my mom. Even right now, even knowing the kind of mood my dad was probably in, the *conchas* made me smile.

I slid up next to him and wrapped my arms around him in a hug. "Hi, Dad."

I was answered with a distracted pat on the shoulder, but he kept staring out the window. I caught Gwen's eyes and sent her a silent message for help.

Gwen cleared her throat. "Hi, Javier!" she said, bounding over. "How's it going?"

My dad blinked and looked up. "Hello, Gwendolyn." One side of his mouth pulled down into a frown, the other side into a smile. Gwen was the only one of my friends who could ever get away with calling my dad by his first name. And my dad, in return, called her Gwendolyn, which she never, *ever* allowed anyone else to say out loud. It was a sort of surrogate father-daughter routine they'd adopted that they both secretly loved.

I gave Dad a kiss on the cheek. That made his frown disappear completely, but he sighed and shook his head, glancing back at the window. "Would you look at that?" he muttered. "A chain, here on Main Street. *¡Qué mala suerta!*"

"Dad, what are you talking about?" I asked.

He stabbed a finger at the glass, and my eyes followed. I loved our quaint Main Street. There were the adorable boutiques and restaurants with bougainvillea-laden terraces. There was the fountain surrounded by bright pink geraniums. But across the street from our bakery I saw something new: Perk Up. It was a branch of the big coffee chain, and it was flying a garish orange GRAND OPENING flag from its front door.

"Whoa," Gwen said, staring. "Something commercially caffeinated this way comes."

"It's so . . . ugly," I said, taking in the sleek metal exterior, the monstrous percolating coffeepot above the store, and the slogan in large letters: GRAB A PERK UP PICK-ME-UP TODAY! On a street lined with mission-style archways and wrought iron, the ultra-modern coffee shop jolted everything out of place. "I didn't even know there was a Perk Up opening here."

Up until today, the storefront had been covered with an "excuse our appearance" tarp. Nobody knew what was being built there. But now the door was swinging constantly, with customers carrying Perk Up's trademark orange coffee cups.

My dad grimaced. "This is the beginning of the end."

"Armageddon is coming to Oak Canyon?" Gwen cried. "Well, I better hurry up with these orders, then." She plunked down at a table, grabbed her jewelry caddy out of her bag, and got to work on her latest pair of earrings. Making handmade earrings and necklaces was Gwen's biggest passion, and her mom had even set her up with an Etsy account. "Can't have people meeting their doom without accessories."

I laughed at Gwen, but my dad's face stayed set in stone. "This is no joke," he said softly.

"Come on, Dad, it's not that bad," I tried. "It's just a coffee shop."

He threw up his hands, and stomped back behind the sales counter. "*Just* a coffee shop. Just a coffee shop that sells coffee worth one dollar for five. It's . . . it's piracy! And meanwhile, the rest of us charge our customers a fair price. And what do we get? Overrun with monopolies!"

I fought the urge to roll my eyes. Occasionally, my dad had a tendency to blow things slightly out of proportion. I followed him through the swinging door that led into the bakery's kitchen.

"Dad, I'm sure Oak Canyon will survive," I said, hoping I could change his mood before something else went up in flames. "Every other town in Valencia County has a Perk Up."

"Exactly," my dad said. "It's the biggest chain in Southern California. No one is going to buy our coffee over theirs, Ali."

I opened my mouth to argue, but then shut it again. He was probably right. We didn't sell Perk Up's type of fancy espressos and mochas; we never had. "But we're not just about the coffee," I reminded Dad.

"True, but who knows what else Perk Up might start selling next." He frowned at me. "If places like Perk Up take our customers, then what happens to us?"

"I don't know," I said quietly, but I didn't like the thought.

My father rolled a tall aluminum baking rack toward me, then pointed to a big mixing bowl full of batter. "Can you get started on the *polvorones*, *cariña*?" he asked.

I nodded and dug into the batter, rolling handfuls into balls, then dipping the balls into a smaller bowl full of cinnamon. I started placing the cookies on baking sheets while Dad tested the oven's temperature. Our bakery was probably the only one in Southern California that used a bona fide wood-burning oven. Yes, my dad hailed from the Stone Age. We had a genuine stone oven, complete with a *bóveda* (domed stone roof). No digital temperature readings for us. My dad could tell the temp just by sticking his arm inside the oven for a few seconds. He called it the art of being a master baker; I called it insanity.

"Maybe it's not chains people want," I said, handing him a tray of cookies ready for the oven. "Maybe they just want something new. Something . . . trendier."

My father slid the tray into the oven and turned around, eyes narrowed. "What are you saying?"

I inhaled sharply, my heart performing triple-flips. Now was my chance. "Maybe we could try something a little trendier, too." I swallowed the thickness in my throat and pressed on. "You know I've been making these cake pops, and the kids at school really seem to like them. . . ."

"Cake pops." He spat the words out, then threw a hand up in the air and marched back into the shop. "*¡Ridículo!*"

"Not ridiculous," I said, my face warming as I picked up on the fact that everyone in the bakery had frozen, hanging on our every word. "Renata DeLuca says they're the most popular dessert for kids under eighteen right now. We could maybe sell some here and —"

"No." My dad cut me off. "That is not the kind of thing we bake here. Our regular customers are happy with what we have."

"Our regular customers are senior citizens!" I cried. I sheepishly looked in the direction of Mrs. Kerny, Mr. Salez, and Mr. Johnson. "No offense," I said to them.

"None taken, sweetie." Mr. Salez chuckled.

"We don't need silly cakes-on-a-stick," my dad continued. "No one here would know what to do with such a thing!"

"I would!" Roberto piped up with a huge grin. "I ate three cake pops this morning."

"Cake whats?" Mrs. Kerny asked blankly.

Gwen snorted a giggle.

"Perk Up, cake pops, landlords," my dad muttered, yanking his apron off and tossing it under the counter. He rubbed his forehead like the whole conversation was giving him a massive headache. "I have to go to PriceCo for more eggs and flour. Rosa, Alicia, could you please watch the store until I get back?"

"Of course, Javier." Abuelita Rosa was already standing up to come behind the counter before I had a chance to say anything. "We'll see you later."

Gwen looked up from her jewelry. "That went well, didn't it?"

"Yeah, right," I said flatly. I watched Dad cross the street to where his car was parked, his shoulders sagging, his gray hair turning silvery in the late afternoon light. Suddenly I thought about one thing he'd said that hadn't made any sense.

"Landlords?" I looked at Abuelita Rosa. "What about landlords?"

Abuelita Rosa sighed and glanced at Roberto, then nodded to Mrs. Kerny to keep an eye on him. She motioned Gwen and me into the kitchen.

She drew her finger through the layer of flour on the baking island, making slow circles and avoiding my eyes.

"Your father found out today that the landlord is raising rent on the bakery," she said. She patted her bun, absently giving it a fresh coat of flour. "That's why he's so upset. It's not just Perk Up. The rent situation. It's . . . not good."

"What do you mean, not good?" My stomach began a slow, wrenching grind. "How much is the rent going up?"

Abuelita frowned. "A few hundred dollars a month. Alicia, the bakery is barely breaking even right now. . . ."

I gripped the counter for support as the floor tilted beneath me. "What?"

"*Lo siento.* I'm sorry," she said. "Your father didn't want you to know. He knew you'd worry. The shop's been struggling for the last year now."

"B-but why?" I stammered. "We always have customers."

Even before she could say anything else, I knew the answer. Yes, we had customers. But they were the same customers every day. We weren't bringing in any new business at all. And we definitely weren't selling out of our pastries and breads, either. None of our breads had any preservatives in them, so they didn't stay fresh long. And how many times had I helped my dad deliver full bags to the soup kitchen in town because we couldn't sell all we'd made?

"Well, Dad needs to talk to the landlord," I sputtered, my mind racing in dumbfounded circles. "We have to do something."

"I don't know what, *niñita*," Abuelita said softly.

"This is dire," Gwen said. "Poor Javier." She squeezed my shoulder. "Poor you."

"We can't close the shop," I said firmly. "We can't. That's not even a possibility. Right?"

I looked from Abuelita to Gwen. Both of them were staring at the floor, speechless. And then Gwen snapped her head up and sniffed the air.

"Um, is something on fire?"

I slapped a hand to my forehead, then ran to the oven. Sure enough, there were the charred remains of two dozen *polvorones*, crisp and smoldering. It was the second time today we'd burned something at Say It With Flour. We'd just set a new record.

Chapter Three

I opened my locker at school the next morning, and an orange slip of paper fluttered to the ground. I picked it up and turned it over. It was a coupon for a free pastry with any drink purchase at Perk Up. I groaned. I'd been trying to forget the bad news, but now everything snapped painfully back into focus.

"Hey," Gwen said, appearing at my side. "So I was thinking . . . do you want to stage a coupon burning protest in the quad at lunch?"

I looked at the fistful of orange papers in her hand. "Where did all those come from?"

"Um, have you looked around?"

I glanced up and down the hallways and saw a sea of orange. Orange flyers were posted on the cement columns, and coupons were falling out of kids' lockers right and left.

"Unbelievable. They're in every single locker," I said. "It's like an invasion. Who put them all here?"

"I'm sure they have lots of minions to do their bidding." Gwen shrugged.

I leaned my head against my locker. "A free pastry with every drink purchase. I didn't even know that Perk Up sold baked goods."

"Yeah, offering free food to a bunch of tweens," Gwen said. "It's genius. Kids are going to be flocking to Perk Up like it's the end of a famine."

She was right about that. Sarah, Lissie, and Harris were clustered in the hallway with their coupons, and I could hear them planning to meet at Perk Up after school.

"They have this amazing chai acai smoothie," Sarah was saying to Lissie. "It's supposed to be great for your skin."

"Oh, this is so bad," I said to Gwen. "Where Sarah goes, everyone follows."

"Hey, I'm not everyone. And I vow to boycott Perk Up products for all eternity."

I nodded, knowing that Gwen meant what she said, and grateful that she'd do that for me.

"You're still looking way too depressed, so I'm declaring a subject change!" Gwen tapped her ears. "What do you think of my latest creation?"

I looked at the blue beaded hoop earrings with the tiny silver hummingbirds dangling in the centers. "I love them," I said. "Can you make me a pair, too?"

"That depends," Gwen said. "Will it cheer you up?"

I smiled. "Definitely."

Gwen's face lit up. "Then absofably, I will. But I think I'll make yours coral red. They'll set off your hazel eyes." The first bell rang, and Gwen patted her bag. "I'll get started on them right now."

"But you have history right now," I said.

Gwen smiled fiendishly. "Exactly. Mrs. Goring is so nearsighted she can't see more than five feet in front of her. And *I* picked a seat in the last row."

I laughed. "Don't get caught."

"Never!" Gwen called over her shoulder as she walked away.

I turned down the hallway, feeling better. But as soon as I got to world science, my mood dampened. Because there was Mr. Cake Pop Killer himself.

As I sat down and reached into my bag for my science textbook, I realized I was still holding that horrible Perk Up coupon in my hand. A fresh wave of frustration hit me, and before I knew it, I was ripping the coupon into shreds.

"So I'm guessing you're not a fan of Perk Up?"

I glanced up into cool eyes the color of mint ice cream. I hadn't noticed Dane's eyes before, but now their bright intensity made it hard for me to breathe.

"No, I'm not," I said shortly. I thought about what my dad had said yesterday about chains, and felt my blood heating up. "It's awful to have some cookie-cutter franchise taking over Main Street."

"Taking over?" Dane gave a laugh. "I'd hardly call one store on Main Street taking over. Besides, Perk Up's profits will boost the town's economy, which is good for everybody, right?"

I stared at him. He sounded like he was quoting something from *Businessweek*, for crying out loud.

"What about the smaller businesses?" I asked. "Some of them . . ." My voice cracked embarrassingly. "Some of them might not survive."

He shrugged. "Well, if the mom-and-pop stores can't stand a little friendly competition, they shouldn't be in business in the first place." Then he leaned closer, studying me. "Why do you care so much about it, anyway?"

"Because my dad owns Say It With Flour," I snapped. "That's why." I glared at him.

Dane raised an eyebrow. "Say It With Flour," he murmured. "You mean the tiny bakery across the street from Perk Up?"

"Not so tiny," I retorted. "My dad's owned our bakery for twenty years. He never had some big chain name to help it along. And he sells *fresh* baked goods made from scratch, not prepackaged Perk Up pastries full of nitrates or MSG, or . . . whatever." I knew I was unloading on him, a boy I'd only just met. But so far, every single thing he'd said had been insulting, or condescending, or both.

Dane smiled, catching me off guard. "Wow," he said. "It's great that you're so passionate about your dad's business. It must mean a lot to you."

I gaped. I was completely disarmed. "It d-does," I stammered.

"It must be nice to not have it just be about money and profit," Dane added thoughtfully.

What does that mean? I wondered. Dane dropped his eyes to his desk, then brought them back up to meet mine. "But there's still nothing you can do about Perk Up. It's in Oak Canyon to stay. Trust me, I know."

"We'll see about that," I said, and then the final bell rang, quieting us both.

"Good morning, ladies and gentlemen," Mr. Jenkins began. "We'll be talking about the anatomy of whales today. . . ."

As Mr. Jenkins lectured, I snuck a look at Dane, wondering what his story was. This new boy was proving to be a big mystery.

Normally, I hated phys ed with a passion. The only plus (and I mean, the *only* plus) was that Tansy and I had it together. Today, though, doing the outdoor obstacle course felt strangely good, like I was sweating out all my frustration.

"Hold up a sec, Ali!" Tansy panted from behind me, where she was still stumbling through the field of tires laid down in the grass. "You're killing me."

"Sorry," I said, jogging in place until she caught up. "I was just thinking about what Dane said earlier."

"Which part?" Tansy asked. "The rude part or the nice part?"

I laughed as we ran to the climbing wall. "When he said there's nothing I can do about Perk Up."

"Yeah." Tansy grunted as she tried to pull herself up the rope and over the wall to the other side.

"But there *is* something I can do," I said. "I can find a way to bring more people into the store. I just have to convince my dad to let me do it." I clambered over the wall and jumped down as a soccer ball flew past my head.

"Heads up!" a voice called out, and Harris came jogging over. The boys always had a separate gym activity from the girls, which was maybe another (small) plus of phys ed.

"Omigod, how embarrassing," Tansy whisper-shrieked. "I'm sweating! He *cannot* see me sweating." She ducked behind the wall while I retrieved the soccer ball from where it had landed.

"Hey, Ali," Harris said, then peered around the wall and grinned. "Hey, Tansy."

"Hey," Tansy's muffled voice squeaked back in mortification.

"Sorry about the stray ball."

"No worries." I tossed it to him. "We needed a breather anyway. Mrs. Stevens has us running the Gauntlet today."

Harris groaned. "Yeah, I hate the Gauntlet. I'm glad Mr. Miller has us doing soccer today. My favorite, obviously." He grinned, started back onto the field, then stopped and turned around. "Hey, are you guys going to the rally?"

Friday afternoon was the Spring into Sports rally, which marked the official opening day for all of the school's springtime sports, like baseball, track, and soccer. Sports aren't my thing, but Tansy is on the school dance team, and they were performing at the start of the rally. Tansy is a fab dancer. It is the only exercise she doesn't mind sweating for. But she always gets horrible stage fright, so Gwen and I promised we'd be there to cheer her on.

"Yeah," I said. "Gwen and I are going to see Tansy dance."

"Awesome!" Harris said. "Maybe we can all hang out afterward."

My heart pole-vaulted into my throat. Harris was asking to hang out? That was a monumental first. Still, I hesitated. "I don't know. I have to study. I'm supposed to have a pop quiz in math next week."

Harris cocked his head. "How do you know when it will be if it's a pop quiz?"

Tansy's laugh came from behind the wall. "Ali's figured out Mr. Kim's schedule. He gives pop quizzes every other week. She'll study every day so she's ready whenever it happens."

I shrugged, giving a little laugh. "I prep for surprises. Can't help it."

"Well, you can still study on Saturday and Sunday, right?" Harris smiled, then started to jog away. "Take Friday off!" he called back over his shoulder.

"Okay!" I called back before I could second-guess myself.

When he was safely back in the middle of the field, Tansy peeked around the corner of the climbing wall.

"Did he just ask you out after the pep rally on Friday?" she whispered, her brown eyes sparkling.

"It was a 'hang out' not an 'ask out,'" I corrected. "That's like the difference between vanilla flavoring and vanilla extract. One is just a tease. Besides, he asked *all* of us."

"Still. That's huge!" Tansy clapped her hands excitedly. "Wait until Gwen hears."

Tansy and I finished the obstacle course on a Harris high, and when Gwen and I left school later that day, it was all we could talk about.

"Do you think it means something?" I asked Gwen for at least the tenth time.

She shrugged. "Who knows? Deep meaning and boys is like an oxymoron. I wouldn't read too much into it. But . . . he could be crushing on you."

"Or Tansy." I nudged her and grinned. "Or *you*."

"Not too likely. I'm too rough around the edges for a boy like him." But the faintest trace of red crept across her cheeks.

"Hey, you're blushing!" I cried, stopping midstride. "Does that mean you *want* him to be crushing on you?"

The hint of red bloomed bigger. "Okay, okay, you outed me." She rolled her eyes in exasperation and sighed. "Let's get one thing straight. He'll *never* ask me out. But if he did, I'd say yes."

"Gwennie!" I hugged her while she grimaced. "You've never said that about any guy before."

She shrugged. "That's because most of them either think constantly about body parts or make noises with them. Yick. Anyway, we don't know who Harris likes. Probably none of us."

"Or all of us," I teased.

"Now you're making my head hurt, which is another reason I don't talk about guys." We both laughed, and I felt lighter and happier than I had all day.

But that was until I got to Main Street and saw a line of kids from school outside Perk Up. They were all holding their coupons in their hands, ready and waiting.

"You've got to be kidding me," I mumbled under my breath.

Sarah, Lissie, and Jane strolled by us in a cluster, each holding a fruit smoothie. Sarah paused in front of us.

"Hi, girls," she said. "You better hurry up and get in line if you want something to eat. They're already out of the cinnamon currant scones. I got the last one."

"Thanks for the tip," Gwen said, "but we're spurning the evil chain today and heading to Say It With Flour, where nothing is mass-produced or shrink-wrapped."

Gwen shot me a "score one for us" look, but then Sarah reached into her Perk Up paper bag and pulled out half of a very fresh-looking, very delicious-looking scone.

"I don't know about the 'evil chain' thing," she said, "but these are homemade and they're an original recipe. Dane made them himself."

"Dane?" I repeated.

Sarah nodded. "Dane McGuire. The boy who just moved here?" She stared at us, then added, "Dane's the one who brought the coupons to school this morning. Didn't you know that his dad owns Perk Up?"

"*This* Perk Up?" I asked, trying desperately to make sense of what I was hearing.

Sarah gave me a tolerant smile, like you'd give a preschooler. "Perk Up, Inc. Michael McGuire owns the whole corporation. How else did you think Dane got permission to advertise on school property? There's no way Principal Dalton's going to say no to the son of a multimillionaire CEO. The McGuires moved here to help set up the new store, but of course Dane's dad doesn't run it himself. He has managers for that." She waved her hand dismissively. "Anyway, Dane's helping out with the baked goods in the store. And they're amazing."

"Oh," I finally managed to say. Suddenly, everything about my talk with Dane this morning made horrible, perfect sense. Except for one thing. Why hadn't he just told me that his dad owned Perk Up?

"Well, see you guys later," Sarah said. She sauntered down the street in all her modelesque glory, sipping her smoothie, a poster child for Perk Up.

And all I could think was: *Score one for Dane.*

Gwen tried her best to cheer me up when we got to Say It With Flour. She even took a break from her jewelry to help me roll out dough for *conchas*. But it was hopeless. I couldn't stop brooding over how Dane had lied to me. Well, not lied. But certainly not told me the whole truth! Not even close.

So, at Gwen's urging, she and I popped over to Perk Up to do some spying. I thought it would be my chance to confront Dane, but he wasn't there. We stood in the endless line, while I took in the sleek, modern (and dull) orange-and-silver décor. Gwen and I ordered a couple of the pumpkin butter gingerbread beignets, which I suspected had been made by Dane himself. Worst of all, the beignets were melt-in-your-mouth magnificent.

When Gwen and I came back to Say It With Flour and shared the beignets with my dad, he went from smoldering to volcanic. And once we started baking, he took his aggravation out on me.

"Sloppiness," he said, grabbing my tablespoon of sugar and leveling it off with a knife. "Alicia, how many times have I told you? Too much sugar spoils the flavor of the *conchas*. Measure *exactamente*."

"I didn't think too much sugar could spoil anything," Gwen whispered.

"Gwendolyn, no, no, no," my dad said gruffly. "That's not right. You don't beat the dough. You knead it. Watch me."

He grabbed a ball of dough from Gwen, examined it, then tossed it in the trash. "It's already ruined."

"Sorry," Gwen said, but my dad just waved us both out of the kitchen.

"Enough!" he snapped. "Both of you! Out, out, out! I'll close up tonight."

So we packed up our school bags and left. And even though I didn't want to admit it, I was relieved. Relieved that I didn't have to see the stress etched on my dad's face anymore, and relieved that I didn't have to stay there while he micromanaged my work. I invited Gwen over for dinner, but she passed. I couldn't remember the last time she'd said no to my grandmother's enchiladas, but she must have needed a break from the tension, too.

Dinner was quiet without my dad, who'd stayed at the bakery late to crunch numbers. I cleaned up the kitchen while Abuelita tucked Roberto into bed. Then I walked into our living room to find my grandmother sitting on the couch surrounded by photo albums. She patted the cushion next to her and I sank down, laying my head on her shoulder.

"I was looking at some pictures of your mother," she said softly. She cupped my chin in her hands and smiled. "She was so beautiful. Just like you, *niñita*."

I ran a finger over a photo of a lovely young woman with a chocolate waterfall of hair and soft, caramel eyes. My mother had become a mystery of sensations in me, a sense of warmth and a cascade of fleeting, blurry images. "I wish I could remember more of her."

"Estrella was full of passion," Abuelita said. "She loved the newness each day brought with it. She used to bake such incredible pastries. She made up all her own recipes. Every week at the bakery there was an Estrella Special."

"I didn't know that," I said. "Why doesn't Dad do that anymore?"

Abuelita sighed, sadness making the lines in her face deeper. "Alicia, we are all like guitars. Our heartstrings stretch to touch others in the universe. And when we think of people with love, those strings sing out, and the song goes on forever, reaching even to those who aren't with us." She closed the photo album. "Your father has tried hard to snap his strings."

I felt a lump in my throat. All I wanted was to send out a song to my mother, and my father. "Abuelita," I said, "I want to help Dad and Say It With Flour."

She kissed my forehead. "Then you will."

She stood up, said good night, and left me sitting on the couch in the dim light, wondering what to do. So I flipped on the TV in the kitchen and found the latest Renata episode. Together, we whipped up a batch of red velvet cake pops with mocha fudge icing.

"What would *you* do, Renata?" I asked the TV screen.

She smiled with her perfect teeth and held a beautiful cake pop up to the camera. "Don't worry if your cake pops don't look exactly like this your first try. With practice, you'll get better.

Remember, the only real mistake you can ever make in baking is giving up."

Her words struck like lightning, and suddenly, I knew I had to try again. This time, maybe Dad would listen. I nested my cake pops into a pastry box, closed the lid, and scribbled a note across the top.

Just try one, Dad. Please.
For the sake of our store.

I laid the box in the middle of his bed, and then I went to my own bedroom and fell asleep, hoping that tomorrow would bring some good kind of newness to all of us.

Chapter Four

When Dad tapped lightly on my bedroom door before sunrise, I'd already been awake for an hour, trying to force myself back to sleep.

"I'm up," I whispered when he stuck his head in the door.

"I could use some help with the cinnamon rolls at the shop," he said, "if you'd like to come along."

"I'll be ready in five minutes." I threw back the covers, wide awake now. My dad never asked for my help in the bakery in the mornings. He was always there long before dawn, heating up the oven and baking the first loaves of the day. Now I wondered why he wanted me to come along, but I knew better than to ask. Dad was like the breads he baked — he needed time to rise to the occasion.

The short walk from our house to the shop was a quiet one, except for the birds chirping out their morning greetings. The bakery sat dark and still, like it was waiting for my dad to open its doors. We lit the fire in the oven, then waited for the fine white crown of ash to form on its arched roof. When the corona appeared, the oven was ready for baking.

We worked side by side until the sun peeked up over the mustard colored hills. Today, my dad didn't loom over my baking, but nodded in approval as I carefully measured the exact amounts of baking powder, flour, and sugar. This hadn't happened in a long time — the two of us sharing the kitchen together without him hyper-controlling every last teaspoon. When I was younger and Mom was still alive, he'd let me create my own doughy concoctions, not caring about the messes I made. Then Mom died and so did our fun in the kitchen. Dad told me that I was old enough to bake in earnest, and as I got bigger, so did his expectations. But today we worked in comfortable silence, and soon I relaxed into the rhythm of the baking.

Finally, we slid the first tray of *bolillos* (the Mexican version of French-style bread) into the oven. Then Dad turned to face me.

"I tried your, uh, cake sticks," he said.

"Cake pops," I corrected.

"Yes, those," he groused. "They are good. Very good." His praise pleased me, but I held my breath, unsure of what would come next. He hesitated, then added, "We can try them in the store."

"Yes!" I grabbed him in a hug, beaming. "Thanks, Dad! They're going to sell, and then —"

My dad held up a finger. "We'll see what happens. We need to bring in new customers. But if your cake pops don't sell, we can't keep them in rotation. Is that understood, Alicia?"

I nodded vigorously. "Yes, yes. But they *will* sell! I know they will." My mind was already humming with ideas for how I could market the pops. With Gwen and Tansy's help, I could even have the word out by this weekend!

I kissed Dad's cheek and his mouth curled into a reluctant smile.

"Enough, enough," he chuckled. "We have work to do."

We turned back to the oven and watched the *bolillos* split their golden sides, their earthy smell filling the shop. It was the aroma that only our bakery (and ours alone) could create in this perfect way. And in its warmth, I always found my mother. This was why nothing could happen to our shop. This was why I would never *let* anything happen to it. And now that I had the go-ahead from my dad to sell my cake pops, I would make sure of that.

When the shop opened for business, I still had some time to get to school. So I sat behind the counter and cracked open my English textbook. Just then, the doorbell tinkled. I glanced up, expecting to see Mr. Salez or Mrs. Kerny, ready for their danishes and coffee. But instead, there was Dane in track pants and a T-shirt, his face flushed and damp. I hated myself for noticing how adorably disheveled he looked.

"H-hi," I managed to stammer, a mixture of irritation and confusion turning my brain to mush. What was he doing here?

A small smile crossed his lips as he pulled his earbuds out of his ears. "Hey." He looked around the shop, taking in the lanterns and the vibrant Mayan rug hanging up over the booths. "Wow, this place is really one of a kind. Pretty cool."

"Thanks," I said, then waited for more. When it didn't come, I finally asked, "So can I help you?"

"Um, I was wondering if I could grab some breakfast to go."

I stared. Wow. And I'd thought he had nerve just setting foot in here.

"Okay," I said, shrugging. "But shouldn't you be buying something from your dad's store instead? Or did you just want to come check out the competition?"

It was a challenge, to see how he'd react. Not the nicest thing I've ever done, but after what had happened yesterday, I couldn't help myself. Now his cheeks turned bright red and his smile disappeared.

"Perk Up doesn't open until eight," he said, glancing down sheepishly, "so you guys have us beat by an hour. And besides, I don't eat my own baking that much. It never tastes as good when you make it yourself."

I knew that was true enough, but I didn't want to give him the satisfaction of hearing me say so. I kept quiet, shooting daggers at him.

He cleared his throat. "So you heard about my dad?" he finally asked.

I nodded. "I was wondering where you got all that business talk from yesterday," I said coolly.

I thought that might embarrass him, but instead he lifted his gaze to look right at me. "I should've told you yesterday," he said. "I just didn't want to make a big deal out of it. Sometimes when people find out who my dad is it gives them the wrong idea about me, like I'm some kind of . . ."

"Evil billionaire?" I finished for him.

He gave a short laugh. "I was going to say stuck-up trust fund kid, but you get the picture."

"Aren't you, though?" I asked. Boy, I was breaking records today for bluntness. If Gwen could only see me now.

He shrugged, and a sudden defiance lit his eyes. "That's not all I am. Besides, being the heir to Perk Up isn't all it's cracked up to be."

I wasn't sure how to respond, and there was a moment of awkward tension between us. Finally, I broke our gaze and gestured down to the counter.

"So," I said, trying to keep my composure, "what would you like?"

His eyes skimmed over the rolls and pastries behind the glass. "What's your favorite?"

"*Niños*," I said. "They're Mexican jelly rolls, super soft and sweet. I have them a lot for breakfast, with hot chocolate on the side."

Dane grinned. "That sounds great. I'll take a roll to go, but I'll have to save the hot chocolate for another day. It's tough to run with scalding-hot liquid in your hand."

I wrapped the jelly roll for him. "Is that why you're up so early? Running?"

He nodded, taking out his wallet to pay for the roll. "I joined the cross-country team. But with the move here, I haven't been running the last couple of weeks. So I've got to build my times back up again."

"Here you go," I said, handing him the bagged roll. And then, because I couldn't seem to keep my thoughts to myself around him, I added, "I hope you like my *niños* better than my cake pops."

He froze, and I was secretly pleased by his shocked expression, even if it only lasted a millisecond.

"You were the one who left the cake pop in my locker?" he asked, then shook his head. "I'm sorry about that. I guess I win the prize for Jerk of the Week."

"It's okay," I said, even though I was still on edge. "I just never knew anyone could hate cake pops so much."

"I don't," he said quickly. "It wasn't that. My dad and I had a big blowup on the way to school. I've been mad about the move, and, well, it had been a banner bad day."

"I've had days like that, too," I said. In fact, my week hadn't started off on such a stellar note, either, thanks to Perk Up. But I didn't think now was the best time to remind Dane of that, when we were finally having a semi-decent conversation.

"Maybe we can start over?" he said. "Pretend like that never happened?"

"Like what never happened?" I blinked, like I'd come down with a serious case of amnesia.

"Thanks, Ali." He grinned. "Well, I guess I'll see you at school."

"Yup. See you."

The door shut behind him, and I watched as he ran down the street. He had his earbuds back in, and he was bouncing off the pavement with each stride. His guarded expression was gone, and he looked almost happy.

"Alicia?" My dad's voice came from behind me. "Who was that boy?"

"A friend from school," I said, and then stopped, rerunning the words in my mind. He wasn't really a friend. Not yet. But there'd been moments when he'd seemed almost . . . nice. There was definitely more to him than the arrogant-seeming rich boy who'd thrown out my cake pop. But still, Dane was the son of the man who was rapidly stealing my dad's business. And I wasn't sure I *should* be friends with him, let alone trust him at all in the first place.

"I need a paper bag," Tansy moaned, fanning herself with her hand while her eyes clenched shut.

"Here we go again," Gwen whispered to me. But then, in true best-friend form, she gave Tansy a supportive smile. "You're not hyperventilating, Tansy," she said. "You're just a little nervous."

I slid my arm around Tansy's shoulders. We'd been in the girls' changing room outside the gym for the last ten minutes, trying to get Tansy to calm down. I kept hoping that Tansy would outgrow her stage fright, but she didn't, so we did this routine nearly every time she performed.

So far today the pep talk was failing miserably, and the Spring into Sports rally was going to start in about three minutes. The loud bass from the speakers was already blasting a hip-hop beat, and the chatter of the kids in the bleachers was reaching a hysterical pitch.

"You'll do fine once you start dancing, like you always do," I said, making my voice as encouraging as possible. "There aren't even that many kids out there."

Tansy gave me a "do I look stupid?" gaze. "There are over *a hundred* kids out there." She put her head between her knees. "Why do I do this to myself? I *hate* performing!"

"But you love dancing," Gwen said. She stood up and grabbed one of Tansy's arms, then signaled me to do the same.

"And everyone loves watching you," I added. We pulled Tansy to her feet and into a three-way hug, squeezing her until she giggled.

"Okay, okay." She shook her arms and legs out, and took a deep breath. "You're right. I've done this before, and I can do it again."

"Thatta girl," Gwen said. "Now get out there."

Tansy gave us a panicky but determined smile, and then ran out the door and into the gym to join the rest of the dance team.

"Well, that's one mission accomplished," I said, then glanced at Gwen. "Are you ready for the second task?"

"Definitely," she said. "Break out the Pops for Jocks coupons!"

I grinned, still loving the tagline I'd come up with. Since my dad had given my cake pops his approval, I'd stocked up on flavored candy chips, colored sugar, cake-pop sticks, and everything else I needed. Last night, in the spirit of the sports rally, I'd baked vanilla-chocolate-swirl pops and decorated them to look like baseballs and soccer balls. They were all sitting at Say It With Flour right now, waiting to be eaten. And the rally was the perfect place to spread the word. I reached into my bag and handed Gwen a big stack of flyers. I took an armful, too, and we headed into the gym, ready to put my plan into action.

We each took half the bleachers, going up and down the aisles with the flyers. "Stop by Say It With Four after the rally and buy one cake pop, get one free," we chanted.

Most of the kids nodded and smiled as they read the flyers, whispering to one another about it. That at least seemed promising.

I finished my half of the bleachers just as the hip-hop beat suddenly morphed into recognizable music, and Principal Dalton's voice came over the loudspeaker.

"Ladies and gentleman, please put your hands together for Oak Canyon's Dancing Divas!"

I slid into an empty spot in the bleachers, then watched Tansy gracefully lope to the center of the gym with a dozen other girls. She launched into a series of calypso leaps across the floor, ending in a half split. She bounced right back up, swinging her hips and kicking her legs in time with the music, no nervousness showing on her face at all now, just happiness.

"She looks awesome," said Gwen, coming up beside me.

I nodded, then glanced down at Gwen's empty hands. "All finished?"

"Yup," she said. "I handed out all of them, so we'll see what happens."

"Well, I made two hundred cake pops," I said. "Either they're going to sell, or I'm going to be eating a *lot* of cake."

Gwen laughed. "Here's to hoping you don't have to eat a single, solitary bite."

Tansy finished up with the dance team and found us in the stands, her face flushed and glowing. Gwen and I tackled her with congratulatory hugs, and then the three of us settled down to watch the rest of the rally. The cheerleading squad was next, with Sarah Chan front and center, her long legs and radiant smile making her impossible to miss. Principal Dalton then called out the sports teams. Every time teams ran onto the gym floor, the cheerleaders made a big show of jumping up and down and leading the bleachers in a cheer. The baseball and softball teams came first, and then came track and cross-country.

My ears pricked up when Dane's name was called, but as I scanned the cross-country lineup, I couldn't spot him. In world science that morning, Mr. Jenkins had split us into our lab groups to study marine fossils. Dane had given me a quick smile as he made his way to his lab station, but we didn't have any chance to talk. And now he was MIA at the rally. I wondered if he was sick or something.

I was about to ask the girls if they'd heard any new info about him circulating the school when Harris's name was announced in the soccer lineup. He jogged onto the gym floor with his team, and I could almost hear an audible sigh from every girl in the room, me included. What can I say? Who wouldn't be a sucker for that adorable, dimpled grin? Even Sarah outdid herself with a sky-high scissoring leap into the air.

Harris waved to the screaming crowd, and for a split second, I thought he looked right at us (or me?), even though we were halfway up the bleachers. My heart skipped involuntarily, and then I immediately scolded myself. What was I doing searching for signals from the guy Gwen had her eye on? That in and of itself felt like some sort of betrayal. Besides, there was no way he'd singled us out of the crowd.

But then, when the rally ended and we were wading our way toward the gym doors, Harris popped up beside me, a posse of his friends in tow.

"Hey!" he said. "Rumor has it there's a new hangout on Main Street we have to try."

I groaned. "I'm sorry, but if you say Perk Up, I'll have to kill you."

"And I'll help," Gwen piped up.

He laughed, then waved my very own flyer in my very red face. "There's this new baker at Say It With Flour. I heard she makes an amazing cake pop."

I couldn't help but grin at his words.

"It's true," Tansy chimed in. "And you haven't even seen her in action yet."

Gwen turned to me. "So let's go now. We can see if our ad campaign worked."

—————————————————————————————

"It definitely worked," I said fifteen minutes later as I stared at the line of kids waiting to get into Say It With Flour. The line that had been across the street at Perk Up had now migrated to our humble little bakery. I felt a swell of pride. "*¡Excelente!*"

I hurried past the line and squeezed through the door to find my dad behind the counter with my abuelita, both of them scrambling to help customers. My dad glanced up from the counter just long enough to give me a tired but beaming smile.

Roberto ran up to me. "Ali! Ali!" he said, yanking on my hand. "Daddy says your pops are selling like hot snakes."

"Hot *cakes*." I hugged my brother.

By that time, Harris, Gwen, Tansy, and Harris's friends had caught up with me. I looked at them all apologetically. "Um, guys, I know we were supposed to hang out, but I need to help my dad. You don't have to stay. You should go do something fun."

"I don't know," Harris said, "this looks pretty fun to me."

Glancing around the bakery with fresh eyes, I realized what he meant. Half the school was here, clustered around tables, laughing and talking . . . and . . . *eating*! Eating my cake pops and everything else the bakery had to offer.

But when I saw Sarah Chan and the triumvirate holding court in a booth, that's when I knew I was making history. Lissie, Jane, and Sarah were each nibbling on a cake pop while giggling about something or other. I blinked with a mixture of delight and disbelief. Harris was right. In one hour, our bakery had become an Oak Canyon hot spot.

"Okay," I said, full of excitement. "Gwen, Tansy, could you keep an eye on Roberto for me?"

"Sure," Tansy said.

Gwen rumpled Roberto's hair. "Hey, squirt, do you want me to pierce your belly button?"

"Yes!" Roberto squealed.

I glared at Gwen, and she held up her hands, all innocence. "Kidding! He can help me fill an order of earrings I have to get out."

"Earrings?" Harris piped up. "Hey, my sister's birthday is next week. Do you think you could make a pair for her, too?"

"Sure," Gwen said, and gave an impish grin. "It'll cost you, though."

"Don't drive too hard of a bargain." Harris matched her smile with his own. "She's only my sister."

Gwen laughed. "I'll show you what I have and you can tell me what you think she'd like." She held up her finger. "But first, we need cake pops." She leaned over the counter and grabbed a batch, ignoring the kids in line who were grumbling and protesting.

"Easy, peeps," Gwen said. "I'm basically family. I have VIP privileges."

She distributed the cake pops among Tansy and Harris and his buds, and they all squeezed into the booth in the far back. Meanwhile, I grabbed my apron and hurried around the counter to my dad.

"Ali, they mobbed us," he said breathlessly as he handed more pops to the kids in line. "The bakery was completely empty and then all of a sudden, this tidal wave."

I beamed at my dad, thrilled to see that his worry lines weren't quite as deep as they'd been this morning. "This is a great start, right?" I said hopefully. "If we keep going like this . . ."

"*Cariña mia*, it's not that simple." Dad put his hand on my arm. "We're not making much profit with the buy-one-get-one-free promo. But maybe, if some of these customers come back again and keep buying more . . ." His voice trailed off as he rubbed his chin, thinking. "Well, for now this is a good sign. A very good sign."

My smile stretched wider. "So what do you need me to help with?" I asked, ready to get to work.

My dad gave a boyish laugh that was wonderfully at odds with his weathered face. "Well, we're going to sell out soon. Is there any way you can make more cake pops?"

I grinned. "Dad, I thought you'd never ask."

Chapter Five

At school on Monday morning, there were throngs of kids clustered around the lockers, but I breezed right past them. It took a full ten seconds before I stopped and swiveled back around, realizing I'd walked past my own locker. And then came the big shocker — the realization that all those kids were hanging around my locker . . . waiting for *me*.

"Hey, Ali!" Harris's friend Tyler gave a friendly wave, and half a dozen other kids said their hellos, too.

"Hey," I said, smiling uncertainly into their expectant faces. I had never been able to lay claim to any sort of popularity at school, so I had no idea what was going on.

"Those banana chocolate chip cake pops yesterday were so yummy," Lissie said. "We were wondering what the special was for today?"

"Oh," I said, a warm thrill rushing through me. Since Friday, Say It With Flour had turned into an overnight sensation. I was making a different recipe every day, and kids had crowded the bakery all weekend long while I frantically made batch after batch. And now they were actually waiting around my locker to find out what the cake pop of the day was? Inwardly, I did a ginormous victory dance. Outwardly, I stayed strictly professional, of course. "Well, today's special is peanut butter chocolate pops with fudge icing."

A collective "Mmmm" echoed through the halls, and the kids immediately started making plans to head to Say It With Flour after school, while I looked on in bliss.

"I'm going to get extra pops for the whale-watching trip tomorrow," Tyler said to me. "We have to bring sack lunches, and my mom always makes me the nastiest tuna melt. I'll definitely need something sweet to force it down with."

He drifted away down the hallway with the other kids just as Gwen and Tansy walked up.

"Were those your adoring fans?" Gwen asked teasingly.

I didn't have time to answer because just then, Sarah Chan herself walked over to join our group, something else that had never happened before.

"Hi there, Ali," she said sweetly, like we were long-lost soul sisters. She tossed her long black hair over her shoulder. "Do you have a sec to chat?"

"Sure," I said, wondering what she could possibly have to chat with me about.

"So I know you all got the e-vite to my party," Sarah continued, glancing at Gwen and Tansy. We nodded in unison. "Well, I'll need a birthday dessert of some kind, of course. And I've tasted your cake pops, which are completely fabulous."

She paused, and my heart clattered wildly. Catering the dessert for Sarah's party would give Say It With Flour a huge boost.

"So," Sarah went on, "I was wondering if you'd like to try out for the job."

"Try out?" I asked, trying to keep my voice on an even keel.

Sarah nodded. "There are two bakeries in town: yours and Perk Up. So I figured it was only fair to let you and Dane both have a shot at catering the party. If he ever decides to come back to school, that is." She said this with exaggerated annoyance, rolled her eyes, and then laughed. "Of course, if I was in Tahoe skiing right now, I'm not sure I'd come back, either."

I gaped at her. "Dane is skiing?"

She gave me a "duh" look, then nodded. "His dad flew him up there for the weekend on the corporate jet." Her laughter tinkled brightly. "If only my dad got one of those with *his* job."

"Yes, if *only*," Gwen repeated in a high, lilting voice. Tansy elbowed her.

Hmm. The ski trip certainly explained why Dane hadn't been around on Friday and why I hadn't seen him all weekend. I'd kept a careful eye on Perk Up, and was thrilled to see that there weren't as many kids from school going in as there had been before. I wondered what Dane would say about "friendly competition" when he got back into town and found out about my cake-pop triumph.

"Anyway," Sarah was saying. "I called Dane on his cell and told him about the catering job, and he wants to try out, too. I just have no idea how I'll ever decide between the two of you. . . ." She gave me a perfect, nearly real smile.

I didn't want to *have* to vie for the job . But I also kind of liked the idea of beating Dane at his own game. Suddenly, a recent episode of *The Baking Guru* popped into my head.

"What about a bake-off?" I suggested.

"A what?" Sarah looked at me blankly, and I realized that for once I was in the know and she wasn't.

"I saw it on a cooking show," I said, my pulse racing. "Renata DeLuca was hiring a new assistant, and she tried out two candidates in front of her live audience. She gave them both identical recipes, and then judged their techniques and the end product."

Sarah's eyes widened. "Ooh, I love that idea." She gave a little golf clap, already acting the part of hostess extraordinaire. "We can have the bake-off the weekend before my party. February ninth. And to make it even more exciting, maybe you and Dane

77

can bake something without a recipe. And all with surprise ingredients! Super fun!"

Suddenly my excitement shriveled into fear. Had she just said something about baking *without* a recipe? My brilliant bake-off idea had taken a very wrong turn. I swallowed down my rising panic, then forced another smile. "Yeah, it does sound like fun," I replied weakly.

"Okay. I'll be in touch!" Then she glided down the hallway, tossing smiles and shiny hair in all directions.

Tansy beamed at me. "Ali, this is incredible!"

"No, this is a nightmare." I grimaced and collapsed against Gwen. "I've never baked anything without a recipe in my entire life. I wouldn't even know where to begin."

"But the bake-off was your idea," Tansy said, blinking in confusion. "Besides, you can make your cake pops, right?"

I shook my head. "I've been using Renata DeLuca's recipes for those. I mean, I tweak them a little bit to decorate them, but they're still her recipes."

"Have you ever tried inventing a recipe?" Tansy asked. "I bet you could do it without Renata. You're good enough."

"No way," I said, shaking my head. "I'm not even close to as good as Renata!"

Gwen gave me her no-nonsense look. "Well, seems to me like you have two options. Back out of the bake-off now, or give yourself a crash course in free-form baking."

"Backing out isn't an option," I said firmly. "The catering job would be great for business, and Dad needs all the help he can get."

"Okay!" Tansy said. "Then let the experiments in baking begin."

I tried to muster up a smile, but I didn't have it in me. Experiments in baking? Yeah right. For someone who hated winging it, it would be experiments in torture.

The next day, I flipped the collar of my jacket up, braced myself against the sharp wind, and stared out at the white-capped waves. Part of me was grateful for the rare chilly day, because at least it would keep me awake.

I'd been up until midnight baking, and I'd kept nodding off

on the bus ride to Long Beach Harbor. Now I stifled a yawn and moved closer to the huddle of kids standing on the pier waiting to board the boats for the whale-watching trip. Sarah, Lissie, and Jane already looked miserable, constantly trying to keep their windblown hair out of their faces, and mumbling about the awful weather. Gwen and Tansy were arm in arm, their faces half buried in their collars.

"Whose brilliant idea was it to go whale watching? I could be in a nice, warm classroom right now, blissfully ignoring Mrs. Waters's lecture on marine mammals." Gwen's voice came out muffled.

"But I love whales!" Tansy said. "Maybe we'll get to see some babies swimming with their moms."

"That would be cool," I said. "My dad told me he used to swim with whale sharks back in Mexico when he was a boy. But he's never been whale watching here."

"Did someone say sharks?" a voice behind me asked, and I turned to see Harris walking toward us. "Now, sharks I'd like to see."

He grabbed Gwen in a joking headlock, and she playfully shoved him away.

"Watch it, Clark," she growled. "Or I'll throw you overboard where you can see sharks up close and personal."

"Careful," I told Harris. "She's a little testy. Suffering from sun deprivation."

He laughed. "And what about you? How did the baking go last night?"

I blushed, pleased that he'd remembered. Yesterday, he and Tyler had stopped by the bakery after school and stayed for a few hours, hanging out with me and Gwen. Harris had introduced us to an online game called *Dragonlore*. It involved a lot of dwarfs and elves and dragon warriors. I thought it was mildly entertaining, but it turned out to be right up Gwen's alley. Harris even asked her to log in later to play with him online from home. At first, I thought it was a sure sign that Harris liked Gwen. But then, a few seconds later, he asked me to play, too. A quick frown had crossed Gwen's face, and I'd instantly excused myself. I'd told Harris that I had three dozen cake pops to make, and then I was going to make my first attempt at free-form baking.

And now here he was, asking about the baking. Even though I could feel Gwen's steady gaze on us as we talked, I was flattered by his interest.

"The baking was hot," I said to him now. "Smokin' hot."

"Really?" He smiled encouragingly.

"Sure." I shook my head. "The kind of hot that requires a fire extinguisher."

He laughed and shrugged. "It was only your first try. You'll get there."

"Well, if last night was any indication, I'll get there sometime next century." I told him how I'd laid out all the ingredients for what should have been a delicious cake, but then I couldn't for the life of me remember how they all mixed together. So I started mixing haphazardly, and when I put the pan in the oven, the batter had oozed over the sides, then bubbled, and then finally erupted. Thus, the fire extinguisher followed by two hours of clean-up detail. Turned out, I'd mistaken baking powder for flour.

When I finished talking, Harris stepped toward me.

"Hey," he said, locking eyes with me in a way that made heat flash across my cheeks. "I'm sure you'll figure it out, Ali."

"Thanks," I said when I could finally find my voice.

Just then, Mr. Jenkins and the other teachers called us to start boarding our assigned boats, and I looked up to see Tansy and Gwen watching me and Harris with wide eyes. That made me blush even more. But instantly, Harris stepped away.

"So, anyway, I wanted to see if you guys could come to our first soccer match on Friday after school," he said, looking at all of us in turn. "The cheerleaders will be at the baseball game, but we could sure use a few people cheering us on, too."

I exchanged glances with Gwen and Tansy, and we all nodded as we started moving toward the gangplanks.

"Great!" Harris said, walking up the ramp to his assigned boat. "See you later."

Gwen narrowed her eyes at me. "Well, well, well, you better spill what just happened back there. It looked like you two had a total moment." Her voice was light and teasing on the surface, but there was a harder edge underneath that made me swallow uncomfortably.

"It was just a 'friend' moment, Gwen," I said. "That's all." I made a big show of rolling my eyes to downplay the whole thing, but the fact was I'd liked how Harris had stood close to me. What I didn't like was the possibility of it souring Gwen's mood. So I grabbed her in a huge bear hug and added, "I mean, he's just a guy, right? Body parts and noises, remember?"

That made her laugh, and I felt better.

"Have fun finding your sea legs!" I called, waving good-bye as I boarded my boat with Tansy.

"Not a chance!" she sang back. But then I saw Harris bop her on the head with a life preserver and a grinning Gwen give him a shove in return, and I was glad to see that, with Harris on board her boat, Gwen might just have some fun on this field trip after all.

Twenty minutes into the trip, though, nobody on *my* boat had found their sea legs yet. The wind was whipping up some impressive swells, and the boat dipped and rocked like a roller coaster. A tame roller coaster, but still, everybody was toddling unsteadily on their feet. We hadn't seen one whale yet, and to make matters worse, some of the kids were starting to look a tad green around the gills.

"Keep your eyes fixed on a point on the horizon and you'll be just fine," the captain urged over the boat's intercom in a voice that was way, way too cheery for the circumstances.

"What horizon?" Tansy moaned, dropping her head onto the railing. "Even the sky is spinning."

"Take some deep breaths," I suggested, patting her back.

But the first deep breath she took sent her running for the bathroom. And within another ten minutes, most of the other kids had disappeared indoors, too. Strangely enough, I felt fine, and I was actually enjoying the steep dips and rises of the boat. The wind and salty air were refreshing, and the ocean looked beautiful, like it had been whisked into a frothy green icing. I tilted my head back and closed my eyes, listening to the roar of the boat slicing through the waves.

"You don't get seasick, then?" a voice asked in my ear.

I blinked, and looked into those unsettling green eyes again. They looked darker today than I'd ever seen them, more the color of the waves.

I hadn't noticed Dane on the pier or boarding the boat, but here he was, watching me with that expression that was daring and dismissive all at once.

"No, I guess I don't," I said. "You don't, either."

He shook his head.

"Did you have fun skiing?" I asked. "I heard you were in *Tahoe* with your dad." It was a test, of sorts, to see if he'd brag about his dad's condo and jet. I didn't know why I always had this urge to challenge him, but part of me needed to see what he'd own up to.

He surprised me with a sudden scowl. "Oh, I'm sure *you* can tell *me*," he snapped. "You probably think I threw a party at my father's pad that he was more than happy to pay for, no questions asked. And that I got lots of time in on the slopes with all my jet-setting friends from Europe, or wherever."

I stared at him. "What? I never said anything about —"

"You didn't have to," he said. "It's all over your face. Rich boy gets whatever he wants on daddy's whim, right?"

"Hey!" I cut him off, my voice rising to the level of the

crashing waves. "Seems like you're passing judgment on *me* right now, too, so lay off. I just asked a question."

His eyes stayed on me, trying to read my face, and I guessed this was *his* test now. To see how honest I was. I must have passed inspection, because he finally dropped his eyes, heaving a sigh.

"I'm sorry," he said. "That was way out of line." He gave me a small smile. "Every time I see you, I feel like I'm apologizing."

"Yeah, well, maybe work on your attitude and that won't happen as much," I retorted, then sucked in a breath. Had I actually just said that? What was *wrong* with me?

But instead of Dane looking angry again, his smile spread. "You're right," he said. He stared out at the ocean. "In answer to your question, my long weekend involved one hour of skiing by myself and about ten hours of mind-numbing business jabber. My dad wanted me to go with him so we could spend some 'quality time' together. Translation: so he could drag me around Tahoe scouting a location for the next Perk Up. So all in all, not such a great trip."

"Ugh," I said. "That sounds pretty awful. I guess I assumed you were going to Tahoe for a fun vacation."

"I know," he said. "Everyone assumes they know about my life. That it must be so terrific to be the son of a man who's made the cover of *Fortune* twice." He frowned. "Did you know we only lived in New Orleans about six months? And before that we lived in Florida, Massachusetts, and Texas? My dad always oversees the openings of the new stores, but once they're up and running, that's it. We're on to the next place."

"That must be hard." I thought about how I'd feel being shuffled from one state to another every few months. Not too great, even if it *was* on a private jet. "Did you leave a lot of friends in New Orleans?"

"I didn't have a chance to make too many in the first place." Hurt skittered across his face and then, just as quickly, he hid it again. "I went out for baseball when we lived in Texas, but we didn't stay long enough for me to play a game." He balled his hands into fists and shoved them into the pockets of his jacket. "That's why I do cross-country now. I'm not letting the whole team down when I have to leave again, at least."

"But," I started, not sure why I felt a little sad, "do you think you might stay here longer?"

"Who knows?" He shrugged. "I'm not holding my breath. But I actually like it here." He met my eyes briefly. "I would much rather hang around Oak Canyon than go skiing alone."

I brushed a strand of hair out of my eyes as a light spray of water misted my face. "So why didn't you stay last weekend, then?"

He let out a short laugh. "My dad doesn't do negotiations. He's priming me to run his company someday, whether I want to or not. He's letting me bake for Perk Up because that was the only way I'd willingly work there. My uncle owns a restaurant in New Orleans, and when we lived there he let me hang out in the kitchen after school. He was around when my dad wasn't. He's the one who taught me how to bake." He sighed. "Anyway, you don't want to hear all this."

"It's all right, really," I said, meaning it. The boat went over a wave that shifted me forward a little, closer to Dane. I quickly took a step back. "I have issues with my dad sometimes, too. He's pretty old-fashioned when it comes to the bakery, and he doesn't want to listen to my ideas, much less use them."

"Yeah, but I heard about your cake pops. They're a big hit." Dane gave me a sideways glance and smiled. "I'm out of town for four days and you pull the rug out from under Perk Up. Pretty impressive."

"Thanks." I grinned, my cheeks flushing. "But I don't think Perk Up has much to worry about."

"So how'd you do it?" Dane asked as we both leaned against the boat railing. "Make the cake pops so huge, I mean?"

I smiled and started talking. And before I knew it, I'd gone from cake pops to my life story. I told him about my mom, and how the bakery was what really kept my dad going after she died. I told him how mad it sometimes made me when my dad acted like he was the only one who knew anything about baking in the entire universe.

"Sometimes I wish that I hated baking," I said, "because then dealing with my dad might be easier. I'd stay out of his way in the kitchen, and he wouldn't always be correcting my every move." I shook my head. "But it's in my blood. I wake up thinking about what I want to bake almost every day. Sometimes I wake up just *to* bake." I dropped my eyes, embarrassed by how ridiculous I was sure I sounded.

I waited for Dane to snicker, or make some smart-aleck remark. But he didn't. Instead, he said, "Yeah, I've got the bug, too. Half the time when I'm supposed to be listening at school, I'm making up recipes I want to try."

"Robert Browning said that when you taste a crust of bread, you taste all the stars and heavens. He pretty much nailed it."

Dane smiled, but then suddenly his face froze staring out at the water. "Hey!" He pointed. "Check it out! Gray whales!"

I scanned the water, but all I saw were endless waves. "I don't see them."

I caught my breath as Dane put his hand on the back of my neck and scooted closer, using his arm as a guide to point them out. "Right . . . *there*!"

And there they were, no more than thirty feet or so from the boat, gliding along in the water, their backs cresting just above the waves. There were two of them, and as we watched, one dove under, its tail flipping up above the water before sliding beneath the surface. The other blew an impressive geyser of spray out of its blowhole.

"They're amazing," I breathed. "So graceful." Suddenly I realized that Dane's hand was still resting on the back of my neck. He'd forgotten it was there. Or at least, I thought he had. He must have realized it at the same second I did, though, because he quickly pulled his hand away, dropping it onto the railing.

He cleared his throat awkwardly while I waited for my runaway heart to slow down.

"Do you know they spend six months of every year homeless?" he finally said, breaking the silence. "They migrate over six thousand miles from the Bering Sea to Mexico and back again. They never stay in one place for very long."

"Sounds pretty lonely to me," I said quietly, watching as the whales slapped their tails against the water.

"It is," Dane said, his voice all certainty. I snuck a glance at him and wondered if he was still talking about the whales.

I don't know how long we stood on the deck, watching the whales perform their water ballet while the wind whipped wildly around us. We were the only two who braved the show. All I knew was that when everyone else dragged themselves off the boats two hours later, pale and moaning, I was smiling, and so was Dane.

I found Tansy and helped her off the boat and tried to hold in my laughter when I saw Sarah straggling down the gangplank looking positively pea green. I had to hand it to her, though, because even in her weakened state, she could still pull off an impressive display of theatrics. Right when she stepped onto the pier, she lost her footing (or pretended to), and toppled straight into the arms of Dane.

"I'm sorry," she said weakly. "I'm just so dizzy."

"No problem," Dane said good-naturedly. "Let me help you to the bus."

As they passed me together, Dane caught my eye for a fleeting second, and then turned back to Sarah. I felt a strange twinge inside me, something almost like jealousy. But I knew that had to be impossible, or insane, or both. After all, Dane was part of Perk Up, and Perk Up was a threat. So just like I'd done with the curious thrill I'd felt when he put his hand on my neck, I dismissed the feeling.

Still, though, on the bus home, I mentally replayed our day. The more I'd talked to Dane, the more surprised I'd been by what he had to say. Slowly, my mental picture of him was rearranging itself, changing from someone stuck-up and spoiled to someone smart, funny, and maybe a little lonely. And I couldn't deny that I liked what I was seeing.

Chapter Six

Harris jogged onto the soccer field with his curls haloed under the floodlights, and Tansy, Gwen, and I all stared. We had to. When you're watching the human equivalent of a triple-layer fudge cake, you don't look away. You savor the flavor.

It was after school on Friday, and the first soccer game of the season. Harris looked up into the stands, saw us standing in the first row, and waved.

"Look at that smile," Tansy said, sighing dreamily. "Ali, I think you're totally front and center on his radar."

My pulse fluttered, but Gwen visibly stiffened.

"Oh, sorry, Gwen," Tansy said, flustered. "I mean, I don't know for sure if he's into Ali. I just meant —"

"No, it's fine," Gwen said briskly. "I've noticed it, too." She followed him with her eyes as he dribbled the ball down the field. "He's tough to read, but he's been making a point of hanging around you."

"I don't know," I said, trying to downplay things. "He's always friendly with all of us." But I wondered if there was some hint of truth to what they were saying. Harris was supernice, and he'd been stopping to chat with me more in the hallway at school, and hanging out in the bakery almost every day. But if Harris did like me, then what about Gwen?

Just the thought made my stomach churn.

Gwen must've seen the worry on my face, because she gave me a playful slug. "Hey, I know the 'all's fair' rule. No need to worry about crushing my futile hopes." She smiled nonchalantly, and I knew she'd never give away how much she liked Harris, even to us. She'd play it off as no big deal.

"If he does like me, which he doesn't," I said firmly, locking eyes with Gwen, "I'd never go out with him."

"But it would be okay with me if you did," Gwen said. "I don't know too many girls in the school who'd pass up a chance to go out with Harris. He's one of those guys you could have as much fun arm-wrestling with as kissing. But you'd have to learn how to play *Dragonlore*, too."

"Uh-uh." I shook my head. "Too many elfin people and goblins . . . not my thing."

"Me neither," Tansy groaned. "All those swords and battle-axes creep me out."

"Hey, don't knock the elves," Gwen said. "I just captured Harris's chief elf, and his magic amulet helped me get to level five."

I laughed, relieved that we'd moved on from the boy talk. We turned our attention to the game. Harris scored a goal, and we all whistled and cheered.

Then Tansy tugged on my arm. "Hey, Ali, what kind of cake pops did you make today?"

"Strawberries and cream with white chocolate icing," I replied. "Why?"

"Because we're surrounded by cake pops," Tansy said, "and they're not yours."

I snapped my head up from the game, and for the first time, studied the other people in the stands. It seemed like every other person was eating a cake pop. They were orange and blue, the Oak Canyon school colors, with a coyote — our school mascot — made out of marshmallow.

"Where did they get those?" I whispered, my stomach tightening.

Gwen didn't waste a second finding out. She went right up to the group of kids closest to us and asked.

"They're at the concession stand," one boy told her. "A dollar each."

"A dollar each?" I cried. "That's half the price of ours."

I started working my way out of the stands and down the stairs.

"Ali, where are you going?" Tansy asked as she and Gwen hurried after me.

"To the concession stand," I said, picking up my pace. "To find out what's going on."

A crowd was waiting in line at the concession stand, and I immediately saw why. A huge banner hung over the top with the words PERK UP POPS! Inside the booth were Dane and a high-school-age guy in Perk Up uniforms, handing out coffees, smoothies, and — yes — bunch after bunch of cake pops.

I let out a gasp and tried to process what I was seeing. Dane was handing out cake pops with a proud grin on his face. Dane, who'd listened to me talk about my cake pops and my family for hours on the boat. Dane, who'd come into world science every day this week with a friendly, open smile on his face, always asking me how I was doing before the bell rang. Dane, who I'd thought was becoming my friend.

Well, I guess I'd been wrong about that, and everything else about him.

As I stood with my mouth hanging open, a couple of kids walked by me, talking between bites.

"These are awesome," one girl was saying. "They taste way better than the ones at Say It With Flour."

"Yeah, and they're way cheaper, too," the other said.

"Oh, Ali, I'm sorry," Tansy whispered, patting my shoulder.

But I barely registered her words through the roaring of rage in my ears. I pushed past the people in line, ignoring their protests, until I was face-to-face with Dane.

"Hey, Ali," he said, smiling casually. "Can I get you something?"

My face burned. Was he kidding? "How about an explanation?" I seethed. "What are you *doing*?"

He shrugged, giving the customers behind me an apologetic smile. "Just doing my job," he said. "That's it."

"That's it?!" I said through clenched teeth. So he wasn't even going to own up to it, then. He was going to act like he hadn't done anything wrong. "You're unbelievable." I spun on my heel and stalked off, fuming.

"Ali! Ali, wait up!"

I didn't want to turn around. I didn't want to hear a word he had to say. But still, my feet stopped against my will, and Dane ran up beside me.

"I'm sorry," he said. "My dad thought it would be a good idea if Perk Up sponsored a concession stand at school events. I know you're surprised. . . ."

"Surprised?" I blurted. "Try furious!" I started walking — okay, stomping — across the parking lot, not caring if he followed or not. "You stole my idea!"

"Wait a second!" Dane grabbed my hand to stop me. "It wasn't your idea! You didn't invent cake pops. And besides, I used my own recipes. I didn't steal anything."

I shook off his hand. "But you made me tell you all about my cake pops and how I promoted them. You used me!"

Dane kicked at the gravel in frustration. "You're not going to believe me, I know, but I wanted to hear about the cake pops because I was having fun talking with you. I thought we could be friends."

"Yeah," I snapped. "You have a weird idea of what friendship is."

"I never said I wouldn't make cake pops for Perk Up."

I scowled. "You're missing the point. You're copying us. What will that do to Say It With Flour?"

Dane stared at the ground, frowning. Then he sighed, and looked up at me. "We are allowed to sell the same product as you, Ali. It's not personal."

"That's the problem," I said. "Nothing is ever personal with you."

I didn't stick around to see what he said after that, if he said anything at all. I walked away, not stopping until I was in the safe cover of darkness under the bleachers. I blew out a hot whoosh of air and sunk down into the grass, trying to cool my broiling face down.

"Hey." Gwen appeared beside me, out of breath, with Tansy on her heels. "We heard it all. Are you okay?"

I swallowed hard, willing myself not to cry. "He is *such* a jerk."

"Maybe he's just under a lot of pressure from his dad," Tansy offered. "You never know."

"Tansy, *please* don't make excuses for him, or I'm *really* going to lose it." Sometimes Tansy's unending rays of sunshine were too much for me. I plucked a few blades of grass out of the ground. "I spent all that time talking to him. And I actually enjoyed it. Ergh! I was so stupid!" I sighed. "Nobody's going to buy pops from us now."

"Could you lower the price?" Tansy asked. "If you made them cheaper than Perk Up's, people would have to buy from you."

I shook my head. "I don't think we can afford to."

"It won't be that bad," Tansy went on. "People love your bakery."

"*And* you can still kick Dane's butt at the bake-off," Gwen added.

I flopped back into the grass. "That's the other problem. My experimental baking is not happening. I have a serious case of baker's block."

"Well, have you consulted the great Renata?" Gwen teased.

I glared at her. "Renata's not helping at all. She makes everything look so easy, but I bet she has a whole team of 'ghost bakers' backstage doing all the hard labor. And I know she doesn't have to worry about Perk Up stealing her fans."

I stood up, drained and defeated. "I'm sorry, chicas, but I'm not in any kind of mood for the game right now. You two stay and enjoy it. Tell Harris I said I was sorry I missed the last half."

"Are you sure?" Gwen said.

"We can come with you," Tansy offered.

"No," I said. "I'll be all right. I'll talk to you tomorrow." I pasted a flimsy smile on my face for show, gave them a wave, and walked away.

The sun was setting in flaming colors behind the hillsides, and the air was turning crisper and cooler. I walked down Main Street, right past our bakery, but I didn't go in. There was no point spoiling my dad's Friday night with the news about Perk Up. After all, maybe Tansy and Gwen were right. Maybe some of our customers would still come, no matter what. We'd know in a few days.

Even though it hurt to know we'd be doing battle with Perk Up again, what hurt even more was knowing that Dane had had something to do with it. I'd really thought we could've become friends. But now I knew that wasn't what he'd wanted. Or — even worse — maybe that was something he didn't know how to be.

"Would you like more tea?" I asked Mrs. Kerny, and I swear my voice actually echoed through the vast emptiness of our shop.

"No, thank you, dear." She looked up from her Sunday paper and smiled kindly. "That's the third time you've asked me in ten minutes," she added in a whisper.

"I'm sorry." I sighed. I'd been wandering around the shop for the last hour, trying to find something to do. But there were no sales to ring up, no plates to wash, no more cake pops to make. No one had come to the shop at all today except for our die-hard loyalists, and the sight of all those empty chairs was completely depressing. My dad had taken up his post by the front window again, watching Perk Up fill with people as our own shop lay eerily quiet. Even worse was that he had told me to only make half as many pops as usual, since on Saturday we'd only sold about a dozen, and he didn't want to waste money on leftovers we couldn't sell. So I'd baked only one batch of cake pops hours ago. There was nothing else to do now.

"Do you have some homework to catch up on?" Mrs. Kerny asked gently.

"I already did it," I said forlornly. "Plus next week's, too."

Mr. Johnson glanced up from his chess board. "Don't worry, sweetie. Things will pick up again. You'll see."

"If you ask me, I like the quiet," Mr. Salez said. "Nice to be able to concentrate without some kid jabbering on one of those cell-doohickeys."

At that moment, the door chimed, and I turned toward the front, hope winging through me. It wasn't the mob of customers I madly wished for, but still, I was happy to see Harris.

"Hi," he said, smiling. "I missed you after the game on Friday, but Gwen told me what happened with the Perk Up pops."

I nodded. "I just needed to get out of there. Sorry I left early."

"No worries," he said. "After what Dane did, you were entitled."

"Thanks," I said, grateful that he understood.

"So," he said, glancing sideways at Mrs. Kerny, Mr. Salez, and Mr. Johnson, all of whom had stopped what they were doing to grin embarrassingly at us, "I stopped by to get a dozen cake pops, if you have them."

"Definitely!" I said too loudly, my face heating up under all the watching eyes. Then I turned to busy myself behind the counter.

"They're for my sister's party this afternoon," Harris said as I packed them up.

"Oh yeah!" I said. "Did Gwen ever make those earrings for her?"

Harris nodded and pulled a box out of his jacket pocket. "I actually just picked them up from her house. Wanna see?"

"Sure," I said, and he opened the box to reveal a pair of turquoise hoops with dragonflies in the centers. "Ooh, those are so pretty!"

"So you think Heather will like them?" he asked.

"Definitely," I said. "Gwen makes great stuff," I added, wanting to put in a good word for her when I had the chance.

"Yeah, she's cool," he said quietly, tucking the box back in his pocket. "I told her she should figure out a way to let kids know about her jewelry at school. She could sell a lot more if she got the word out better."

"I bet you're right. I'll see if I can brainstorm some ideas with her. Here you go." I handed him the cake pops, which I'd wrapped in a pink ribbon to make look like a pretty bouquet.

"Thanks," he said. "And, Ali? For the record, your cake pops are still the best."

"Thanks," I said, blushing furiously.

He gave me a sweet smile that made me blush more and then, with a shattering rain, I dropped his change all over the counter.

"Oops." I giggled, then scrambled to recover the spinning coins.

"No problem." He helped me collect his change, then turned toward the door. "I'll see you at school tomorrow."

I nodded and waved, but the second he left the store, a leaden guilt settled over me. How could I let the boy my best friend liked make *me* that flustered? I so needed to get a grip. I scurried around behind the sales counter, fumbling for something to do. But after a few minutes of failing miserably, I gave up and sank into a chair with a sigh.

Dad must have picked up on the frustration in that sigh, because he came over to me.

"Vete," he said, giving me a quick kiss on the forehead. "Go take the rest of the day off. It's slow again this afternoon, and there's no reason for two of us to sit around feeling sorry for

ourselves." He said it in his Eeyore voice. It was the voice he'd had as long as I could remember, but when my cake pops had taken off, he'd lost it. Only now it had returned again with a vengeance.

I wanted to tell him to snap out of it, not to give up. But I didn't have the heart to fake it, either. So I quietly nodded, then picked up my school bag and headed for the door.

"Call Gwendolyn or Tansy and do something fun!" he hollered after me.

But I didn't feel much like hanging out with friends. Instead, I went home and snuggled on the couch with Roberto to read some books. After the third picture book, Roberto fell asleep, his mop of curls tucked under my chin. So I nestled deeper into the couch and turned on the latest episode of *The Baking Guru*.

I was still sitting there an hour later, jotting down Renata's recipe for apricot popovers in my notebook when Abuelita Rosa came in from the kitchen. She cuddled up next to me.

"How was the bakery today?" she asked.

I groaned. "Deserted. Dad told me we can't lower the price of our cake pops, so half the town is camped out at Perk Up again."

She nodded, clucking her tongue. "It's a shame. But you might still be able to turn the tide."

I sighed. "Dane has the advantage."

Abuelita studied my face. "How so?"

"He comes up with his own stuff," I said. "I just use Renata's."

"Ah, well, that can be fixed with time."

"I don't think so," I said. "Whenever I try to come up with something on my own, it falls apart. I'd have to find a way to give my cake pops something special . . . something his don't have."

"And you will." She smiled and brushed my hair back from my face. Then she stood up, a glint of mischief in her eyes. "I have something for you. I'll be right back."

I watched her go, wondering what she was up to. A minute later, she returned, holding a worn clothbound book in her hands. "This," she said, sitting down next to me again, "was your mother's recipe book."

My eyes widened as she slid the book into my lap. I held it tentatively, afraid that it might wisp away into thin air at the slightest touch.

"But where did this come from? I didn't know she had a recipe book. . . ."

"I know." Abuelita sighed, her lips pursing like they did when she was trying to hide her irritation at something. "When your mother left us, your father put her things away. He didn't want reminders around the house. He said it wasn't good for you and Roberto. But really, it wasn't good for him. He didn't like the pain that came with seeing her jewelry, her clothes, or this." She patted the recipe book gently. "He gave everything away. Or thought he did. I saved a few things that I thought she'd want you and Roberto to have some day. This book, I saved for you."

I stared at its faded yellow cover, its fraying and dented spine. I opened the book, and saw that the first page was filled with a lovely, fluid cursive. *Recetas por Estrella*, it read. *Recipes by Estrella.* Sudden tears burned at the corners of my eyes. I hadn't seen anything belonging to my mother in years, and I wasn't ready for the pang of longing that came with it.

"I told you that your mother made up her own recipes," Abuelita said. "Now you can read them for yourself. Try them, if you want. Maybe you'll find something that inspires you."

"This is amazing," I whispered. "*Gracias*. Thank you."

"You're welcome." She wagged a finger at me, her eyes playful but serious all at once. "Now, your father doesn't know we still have this. Let's you and I sit with it for awhile, before we show him. No use getting him all in a huff when he has so much to worry about already. *¿Comprende?*"

"*Sí, sí,*" I said. "Yes." I was already itching to read the whole book.

I went into my room, curling up on my bed with this treasured secret. My mother's book. I carefully opened it, feeling the fragile crackling of the pages between my fingers. There was the first recipe, one for *pastel de dulce de leche*, caramel cake. I read the two-sentence description:

Make this cake on days when you can't find your smile.
Eat it warm with fresh cream drizzled over the top.
and you'll find the sweetness in things again.

I brushed my fingers lightly over the words, marveling that my mother's fingers had once touched the same paper. I put my nose close to the paper and breathed in, and I thought I could smell the faintest trace of chocolate and . . . was it roses? I smiled, turned the page, and kept reading.

Chapter Seven

"Is it done yet?" Gwen asked for about the fiftieth time. She and Harris peeked around the door of the kitchen. "Just the smell has got my mouth watering."

"Not yet," I practically growled, but I couldn't blame her for her impatience. The cooling cake on the counter had a rich caramel-cream scent with cinnamon undertones.

Wednesday afternoons were when my dad always did the shopping for supplies, so I had the bakery to myself after school, and I was using it to try out my mom's first recipe.

"Please give her some," Harris told me. "Little Miss Impatient is getting violent with my Benzoian Dwarves. If you don't feed her soon, she's going to take them all to the dungeon for torture."

Gwen slapped his shoulder. "You're such a crybaby. You held my Alpha Dragon hostage for a week and cost me three thousand rubelitts in ransom money."

I waved them out of the kitchen. "If you two don't get out, nobody's getting a single bite!" I yelled in mock anger. "Let me finish!"

Harris ducked out shyly while Gwen stayed long enough to stick her tongue out at me before letting the door close. I turned back to my work, crumbling the cake and adding in icing to shape it all into cake balls. Then I let the balls cool in the freezer before adding the pop sticks and dipping them in caramel candy coating. To finish off the pops, I rolled them in white chocolate chips. Finally, when they were done, I brought two pops out to the front and handed them to Gwen and Harris.

"Be brutally honest," I said, then watched as they both took generous bites.

"OMG," Gwen said, closing her eyes and smacking her lips. "Perk Up's got nothing on this!"

I grinned. "That's the idea."

Harris took a bite. "There's something different about it. It's kind of tangy, or citrusy, but in a really good way."

"Mandarin oranges," I explained.

"Weird," Gwen said. "But my taste buds thank you!" I laughed as she finished the rest of her pop in a single bite. "Did your mom make up more recipes like this?"

"A ton," I said. "Her book is full of them. And most of them I can make into cake pops super easily." I moved Gwen's jewelry caddie over to make room at the table, then sat down with them. "I'm not sure it will help the bakery, though. Dad told me last night that he might pull the plug on the cake pops unless we start selling more of them again."

"You need to find a new way to bring customers in," Harris said. "If kids can get cheaper pops at Perk Up, that's where they're going to buy them."

"Don't remind me," I said, dropping my head onto the table. For the last three days, I'd basically been avoiding all things Dane, which was challenging, considering his seat in world science was only about a foot away from mine. Still, I'd managed to strategically keep my eyes glued to my textbook or on Mr. Jenkins through the entire period. I could sense Dane's eyes on my face a few times, and he'd even slid a piece of paper onto my desk that said "Sorry." But I didn't give in. I just couldn't be friends with him after what had happened. It felt too much like a betrayal to my dad. And if there was one thing my dad didn't need right now, it was his daughter joining forces with the enemy.

"Anyway," Harris was saying, "what I meant was, you could give kids another reason to come into Say It With Flour. Maybe something other than food. Something fun."

I ran my fingers across the necklace that Gwen was working on — a blue-and-green beaded choker with a glass medallion. And suddenly, inspiration struck. "Hey, instead of getting kids to come here after a big event, why not have a big event here?"

Gwen and Harris looked at me blankly.

"We could have a jewelry show here!" I said, a jolt of excitement racing through me. "We could invite all the eighth-grade girls. Gwen, you could sell your jewelry, and I'll sell my cake pops." My thoughts were racing with possibilities. "I bet all the girls would be into it! Even Sarah would come."

Gwen raised her eyebrows skeptically. "Sarah Chan come here to buy my jewelry? That's like Kate Middleton shopping in a dollar store."

"Are you kidding me?" Harris elbowed Gwen. "My sister Heather is a senior in high school and loved your earrings. Maybe she could even post a picture of the earrings on Twitter."

"We can hype up the party on Facebook, too. Send out e-vites." I smiled at the thought of girls streaming through the bakery doors. If this idea worked, it could put us back on the map. "We could call it something really cute. Maybe . . . Bling and Bake?" I suggested.

Gwen's eyes lit up. "I love that! There are, like, sixty girls in our class," she said, and I could see her mind churning over the figures. "I need at least a week to get enough pieces ready."

"That's okay," I said. "We can have the party a week from this Saturday. That'll give us a week and a half to get ready. I'll have to check with my dad, but I'm sure he'll say yes. I need time to work through my mom's recipe book, too. I want to pick out the perfect recipe for the show."

Gwen narrowed her eyes at me. "What about trying your own recipe? Aren't you supposed to be practicing for the bake-off?"

I waved her question away. "I'm not going to risk messing up this big event with off-the-cuff baking. That would be stupid." I shook my head. "I'll use my mom's recipes for the jewelry show, and worry about the bake-off later."

"Okay, whatever you say," Gwen said, but she saw right through me, just like she always did. She knew I was chickening out. And she was right. The fact was, I didn't want to subject myself to more disastrous baking meltdowns when I could use my mom's book instead.

I stood up. "I still have time to try mom's recipe for apple streusel cake before my dad comes back. I should get started."

Gwen nodded. "I should go to the craft store to get more earring posts and beading wire." She stood up, then smiled. "If this wasn't going to be so much fun, Ali, I'd say you were exploiting my supreme talents for your own advancement."

I grinned. "And if you weren't my best friend, I'd say the only reason you came to the bakery every day is for the all-you-can-eat cake pops."

Gwen clutched her chest. "Oh, you've found out my deepest, darkest secret!" She lurched to the door and fell through it, playing up the drama while Harris and I laughed. "I'll be back later for more pops!" she called as she walked down the street.

"She's a lunatic," Harris said, smiling as he shouldered his backpack.

"That's why I love her," I said.

He looked at me, his velvet eyes suddenly serious. "You know, you're a really good friend to Gwen. The jewelry show idea is great. I bet it's going to be huge."

"I hope so," I said. He seemed ready to say good-bye, but then he took a step toward me, ducking his head awkwardly to stare at the tiled floor. I'd never seen Harris looking so unsure of himself before, and heat flashed over my face. *Please*, I pleaded silently, *let this not be what I think it is.*

"Ali," he mumbled, his eyes still locked on the tiles, his cheeks sunset red, "um, I was wondering if you —"

The doorbell tinkled, and both of us jerked our heads up at once.

"Oh, excuse me, dears," Mrs. Kerny said, her eyes sparkling as she took us in. "I didn't mean to interrupt. I was just coming in for my afternoon tea."

I spun to the counter, nearly toppling a chair in my hurry. "Of course! I'll get it right away." I scrambled to get the tea, too flustered to make any sort of eye contact with Harris again.

"I better go," he muttered, waving in my direction. "I'll talk up the show to Heather and see if we can spread the word."

"That would be great," I said, supremely thankful that we'd moved past the awkward moment. "Thanks."

After he was gone, I carried the tea to Mrs. Kerny. I hoped she'd think that it was my clumsy footwork making the teacup rattle, and not my shaking fingers. But of course, she was watching my every move with eagle eyes.

"So you have yourself a little beau." She chuckled as she scratched her Chihuahua, Bambi, under the chin.

"Oh, no, no," I stammered, setting the tea down, miraculously without spilling a drop. "He's just a friend."

"Mmmm." She took a sip of her tea, her eyes never leaving my face. "I had a friend like that once." She winked at me. "He became my husband."

I giggled nervously and backed away until I was safely behind the counter again, where I focused on arranging plates and silverware. But even though my hands stayed busy the rest of the afternoon, my mind kept coming back to Harris. Had he been about to ask me out on a date? No. Maybe he'd only been trying to ask me about the weather, or math homework, or something else completely ridiculous.

Yes, that had to be it, I told myself. Because things among me and Harris and Gwen could *not* get any more complicated. Sure, I liked the way he smiled, and I thought he was fun. But it had to stop there. There was no way I would hurt Gwen by going out with him, even if she did say she was okay with it. But if I said no, then would things be weird between Harris and me? And in my heart of hearts, was "No" the answer I really wanted to give him in the first place? *¡Caramba!* This all made my head hurt.

And right now, I had way too much else on my mind to try and figure it out.

I thought I had a lot on my mind Wednesday, but by Thursday afternoon, my brain had gone from sautéed to flambéed. The final bell had rung, and I'd just said good-bye to Tansy in the girls' locker room. I wound my way down the dirt path that led from the gym to the sports fields, hoping to take the shortcut to get to Main Street. I told myself that I wasn't walking this way to try to catch a glimpse of Harris playing soccer. But my jittery stomach told a different story.

When I rounded the base of the hill where the bleachers stood, though, I didn't see Harris. Instead, I saw Dane. The rest of the cross-country team was breezing by him, but Dane was standing at the edge of the track, his arms crossed, his face tight with anger. And I knew why. He was talking — strike that — arguing with a man in a dark suit standing next to him. His dad, I realized, recognizing him from that first day when Dane arrived in the limo.

I quickly ducked behind the bleachers, planning to backtrack to the gym before Dane saw me. The last thing I wanted was an awkward encounter with Dane, who I still wasn't speaking to, or his dad, who I'd never officially met. But then I heard "Say It With Flour," cross his dad's lips, loud and clear. I froze, hating myself for eavesdropping, but not able to tear myself away, either. I peered through the slats in the underside of the bleachers, holding my breath.

"Look," his dad was saying, "I know I've been preoccupied lately, but that little bakery is putting a dent in Perk Up's opening-month sales."

"Are you kidding me?" Dane's voice was hard-edged. "So you're missing my cross-country meet tomorrow because you're worried about Say It With Flour?" He kicked at the track, scowling. "That's the lamest excuse I've ever heard."

"You're missing the point," his dad said. "Even one customer lost to that run-down place is one too many. I have to fly to Boston to meet with the corporate team to figure out some new strategies. There will be other track meets." He gave a smile that looked way too practiced to be real. "Besides, that's why I stopped by today. To watch you train for tomorrow."

Dane laughed, but the sarcasm and hurt in it made me cringe. "Don't bother staying, Dad," he said, stepping back onto the track. "You should go back to your office and crunch those numbers. They're all that's important, right?"

With that, Dane shot down the track, leaving his dad in a cloud of dust. I willed his dad to stay, or maybe even to catch up with Dane on the other side of the track. But instead, his dad cleared his throat and straightened his tie. As he walked toward the parking lot, his cell phone rang, and he answered it, without ever looking back.

I edged around the bleachers tentatively, hoping that Dane was a safe enough distance away that he wouldn't see me. I didn't need to worry about that, though. His eyes were unwavering, staring straight ahead, as he caught up and then smoothly blew by most of his teammates. I noticed Sarah and Jane sitting in the bleachers on the other side of the track, watching him. Sarah's enthralled smile made it seem as if cross-country were the most riveting sport in the world to her. But her avid attention was completely lost on Dane. He never turned his head in their direction. He just kept running, right off the track and onto the dirt path climbing into the hills behind the school. Soon he caught up with Jake and Toby, the two lead runners. I'd seen him hanging out with them at lunch lately, and now they nodded and exchanged a few words. But even they couldn't keep up with him. Dane looked comfortable up there by himself, like he was used to being a loner, and he wasn't expecting his status to change anytime soon.

I watched him until he disappeared over the crest of the hill. Then I turned toward Valencia Avenue, my thoughts a whirlwind of confusion. I didn't want to care what happened between Dane and his dad. I should've been thrilled to hear that Say It With Flour was putting a damper on Perk Up's sales. But when I thought about the disappointment and anger on Dane's face, I couldn't enjoy what I'd overheard. Maybe I did care what happened to Dane. Maybe more than I was willing to admit.

Whatever the case, I had discovered one inescapable, inarguable truth: Businesses and boys caused a lot more trouble than they were worth.

Chapter Eight

"Shouldn't the sign be a little higher?" I asked, staring up at the Bling and Bake banner hanging across our bakery awning.

Gwen glared down at me from her perch on the ladder. "Hey, you worry about your cake pops, I'll worry about my banner."

I laughed. Gwen always got grumpier when she was nervous.

"You know there's nothing to worry about," I said. "The show's going to be fab." For the last week and a half, we'd talked up the show on our Facebook pages, and Harris's sister Heather had raved about her earrings on Twitter. It worked like magic. At school, the jewelry show had almost trumped Sarah's upcoming birthday bash in hallway chatter. Sarah and the triumvirate had all RSVP'd a resounding yes, and so had almost all of the other eighth-grade girls.

"It won't be fab if we're not ready in time," Gwen quipped. "So go put your baking genius to work."

"I'm going," I said, scooting through the door before she got violent. Inside the bakery, my dad and Tansy were decorating the shop, laying down tablecloths and setting up Gwen's jewelry displays. It was still morning, but we had a lot of work to do to make everything perfect by the time the show started at two.

"Looking good," I called, then hurried to the kitchen. There, two cooled, crustless Mexican chocolate cheesecakes were waiting for me to transform them into glam cake pops. After trying out different recipes in my mom's book for the last week, I'd finally decided on her cheesecake for the jewelry show. Luckily, my dad didn't think to ask where I'd suddenly gotten my inspiration, but I was careful to keep my mom's book tucked in my backpack most of the time, just in case. This recipe used authentic Mexican chocolate and a dash of cayenne pepper, and I was adding a morello cherry center to each pop for extra oomph. My plan was to mold the cheesecake into balls around each morello cherry, chill them, and then decorate them.

I was just scooping up the cheesecake to make the balls, when my dad stuck his head into the kitchen.

"You have a visitor," he said.

"Okay," I said absently, keeping my focus on the pops. "Just send them back here."

My dad nodded and disappeared, and the next time I glanced up, Dane was standing in his place.

"Hi," he said quietly, taking in the counter strewn with cherries, cake, and candy chips. "Wow, that looks impressive. Is that for the Bling thing?"

"Yup," I said coolly, not taking my eyes off the pops.

"It's a brilliant idea," he said, and I thought I heard a smile in his voice. "My dad's totally peeved that the manager at Perk Up didn't come up with something like it first." He gave a little laugh. "They're brainstorming as we speak."

"Great. It'll be so much fun to see what they come up with," I practically growled. I mean, did he *really* think I wanted to hear that Perk Up was planning on taking another one of my ideas? Come on.

"Hey," Dane said, stepping closer to force me to meet his eyes. "You don't always have to get so defensive, you know. I wasn't trying to start a fight, I was just making conversation."

"Well, maybe if you didn't bring up Perk Up constantly, you might get a better response."

I gave him what I thought was an intimidating glare, but he laughed. "True enough." He tucked his hands into the pockets of his jeans, and I could see the tips of his ears reddening slightly under his blond waves. If I hadn't known him better, I would've said he almost looked nervous. "Anyway, I know you're busy, so I'll only stay a second," he went on quickly. "I wanted to see if maybe we could call a truce. I'm not sure we're ever going to agree when it comes to our parents' stores, but maybe we can still be friends. Or if not friends, maybe we could sit next to each other in world science without you shooting death rays in my direction?"

The giggle surprised me, popping out of my mouth before I had any idea it was even there. I tried to hide my smile in my sleeve, but he caught a glimpse of it before I could. And he smiled back. After all, he did have a point. I hadn't cut him any slack over the last two weeks. Maybe he didn't deserve it, and keeping up the grouchy act was getting pretty tiring, too. I wasn't naturally mean-spirited, and holding on to that anger all the time didn't feel good.

"Ali!" Gwen's blaring voice from the front of the shop made me jump. "Your dad isn't letting me move the Mayan rug, and it's not really working with the trendy Bling look. Help!"

I held up my finger to Dane. "Can you wait here a sec? I'll be right back."

I ran out to the front and refereed between Dad and Gwen until Dad grudgingly tucked the rug under the counter. When I got back to the kitchen, Dane was still there, his eyes a hopeful question mark.

I suddenly remembered the talk I'd overheard with his dad yesterday. That only furthered my desire to put all the fighting behind us.

"All right," I said. "Truce."

"Great!" His face broke into a wide grin. "So maybe that means you can help me study for our test on marine mammals, too?"

I was about to tell him not to press his luck, when the kitchen door swung open and Sarah and Lissie sashayed in like Oak Canyon's most desirable VIPs. I stared. Sarah hadn't set foot in the bakery for weeks, and the show didn't start for another four hours. I knew she didn't do anything without a purpose. So what was she doing here?

"Did I just hear you say you needed help studying for your world science test?" Sarah gave Dane a dewy-eyed glance. "You know, I have the highest grade in Mrs. Waters's class. I could help."

"Thanks," Dane said. "I'll think about it."

She leaned over the cheesecake spread on the counter. "Mmmm," she said with exaggerated enthusiasm, "doesn't that look delish? And speaking of delish, I found the perfect dress for my party at Ooh-La-La's. My dad's on his way over with the credit card, but since I was waiting, I thought I'd drop in to give

Ali the details of the bake-off. I had no idea you'd both be here! How lucky."

"Sure thing," Dane said. "Fill us in."

"So you already know you'll be baking cake pops." She smiled. "I'll provide all the mystery ingredients. And we'll have a panel of random judges do the taste-testing and voting."

"Sounds fun," Dane said cheerfully, as if it was the easiest thing in the world for him to toss random ingredients together to bake a masterpiece. I gave an involuntary shudder. If only it were that simple for me, too.

"Oh, and we're holding it at Oak Canyon Community Park, February ninth," Sarah added, already turning back to the door. "My dad wanted to invite a few people, so you'll have a small audience. But that shouldn't be a problem, right?"

"No problem," Dane said casually.

"No," I said quietly, feeling my hands turn clammy at the thought.

"Super," she said, linking arms with Lissie. "See you later this afternoon, Ali! We can't wait! Oh and, Dane, don't forget to call me if you need help studying." Then she was gone, trailing a cloud of lilac body spray behind her.

I tried to swallow down the rising dread I felt about the bake-off, hoping my nervousness wasn't written all over my face. I hadn't had much time to think about it lately, since I'd been so busy planning the Bling and Bake. But leave it to Sarah to remind me at the worst possible time. I turned to the sink to rinse off my hands and let the cool water calm me down, and there was Dane, by my side, peering at me with those inquisitive eyes. I got the feeling that even if he wasn't saying so, he could see right through me.

"I guess I'll head out, too," he finally said, breaking the silence. "I'm glad we got to clear things up. But . . . do you think we'll still be speaking to each other after the bake-off, or should I plan on this being a temporary cease-fire?"

I smiled. "I'm a baker, not a fighter. Let's make it permanent."

"I'd like that." He held out his hand for a shake. I slid my hand into his, and then felt a thrilling surge of warmth pass through my fingertips. We both pulled away quickly, and I wondered if he'd felt the same thing.

"I know you don't need it, but good luck today," he said at the door. "I hope the show is a big success, and I mean that."

"Thanks," I said. "I'll tell you about it on Monday in class."

He waved and disappeared, leaving me staring after him in a daze, wondering what exactly he'd become. A friend? A frenemy? Who knew? My mind was screaming at me to proceed with caution, but my heart . . . my heart was holding on to the feel of his hand in mine. I shook the feeling away, vowing not to lose myself in some ridiculous daydream about a boy I could barely stand.

It was true that I could barely stand him, wasn't it? Of course it was! I needed to refocus on the Bling event.

On cue, Tansy called out, "Ali, your dad just left to run errands. Can you please come help us move some tables?"

I rushed out of the kitchen, grateful for the distraction. In fact, I focused so completely on rearranging the furniture that I barely registered when Sarah came rushing back into the store.

"Sorry!" she called out as she made for the kitchen. "I left my cell in the back. Be just a sec!"

When she came back through the shop a few minutes later, she was smiling. "I ran into Dane outside, and he wants to study with me after his shift ends at Perk Up." She held up her cell. "Wouldn't want to miss his call! Later, ladies!"

"Interesting," Gwen said after she'd gone. "Sounds like she and Dane are getting cozy."

"They're just studying," I said, sounding more snappish than I'd intended.

Gwen raised her eyebrows in surprise. "Okay, okay, no need to get touchy."

"I don't really think Sarah's his type anyway," Tansy said with a small smile as she fixed a necklace display.

Gwen nodded. "You know, once in a brief moment of madness, I actually thought Dane would be perfect for you, Ali." She snorted. "Ridiculous, right? I mean, you guys can't be around each other for more than two minutes without fighting."

I laughed shortly, but my heart was racing. "Yeah, absolutely ridiculous." But Gwen's eyes stayed on my face longer than usual, and I quickly escaped to the kitchen. I leaned against the cool fridge door, fanning myself. What was that all about? I wasn't even sure I knew myself. But I did know one thing: I had two hundred cake pops to finish in four hours, and all this Dane drama wasn't helping. Not one bit.

Matter over mind. That was my motto for the rest of the day. I pushed Dane, *and* Sarah, *and* the bake-off all out of my mind, and honed in on matter. Or, batter, actually. Five cheesecakes' worth of batter. And I got the pops done, with an hour to spare.

"They're works of art," Gwen said when I brought them out into the shop in bouquets tied with silver and gold ribbon. "Seriously. Like little Renoirs on sticks."

I laughed. "I wouldn't go that far. But they look good, don't they?"

"They're adorable," Tansy said.

"Thanks," I said, beaming. I'd dipped each pop in a bowl of melted pale-pink candy bits and added tiny gold-and-silver neck-laces and earrings with metallic icing. I think I took extra care because my hands were working now where my mom's had worked so long ago. When I baked something of hers, I got the feeling that somehow she was guiding me, helping me. My mom's recipe book was proving to be a lucky charm.

"Everything looks incredible," I said, glancing around. Tansy had made colorful geranium arrangements, which were scattered around the shop among the jewelry. Gwen's necklaces, earrings, and bracelets were displayed proudly on white tablecloths, looking very professional. Best of all, there was already a line of girls outside.

Gwen snapped her fingers. "Let's get this party started!" She ran to open the door while I took my place behind the counter with my dad, ready to start selling cake pops.

Girls flooded into the store, squealing and chatting as they browsed through the jewelry. Sarah, Lissie, and Jane all bought earrings and necklaces right away, and other girls quickly followed their lead. It was one of the few times I was genuinely grateful that Sarah was such a trendsetter. Within ten minutes, Gwen had already sold a dozen pieces of jewelry and Dad and I had sold thirty cake pops.

I was starting to have visions of success that far exceeded my original expectations.

And then Jane let out a heart-stopping scream of terror.

Everyone in the store froze, and all eyes turned on Jane. Suddenly, the one scream turned into dozens. Because out of Jane's mouth came an oozing black liquid, like something right out of a horror movie. And she wasn't the only one. All the girls who had bitten into their cake pops had mouths dripping in black.

My heart stopped.

"Oh, gross," Tansy shrieked. "What is that?"

"I have no idea," I said, rushing around the counter with glasses of water. But most of the girls had raced for the bathroom and were in there trying to wash their mouths out at the sink.

"It's not coming out!" Lissie shrieked, pointing to her blackened tongue and teeth.

"It's like a 90210 version of the black plague," Gwen said. She was trying hard not to smile, and one warning stare from me wiped the hint of it right off her face. "Sorry. What do we do?"

"Damage control," I said. "Start asking around to see if anyone has toothpaste. Right now."

Luckily, Sarah had toothpaste in her bag, but even that didn't get rid of the black tint all the way. By now, a lot of the affected girls were crying, while the ones who hadn't yet tasted the pops were trying, and failing, to be comforting.

"It doesn't look that bad," Sarah, who'd escaped unscathed, was saying to Lissie. "In a few days, it'll be gone. A week at most."

That made Lissie wail louder.

I apologized over and over again, but what I was apologizing for, I didn't know. What had possibly gone wrong? I hadn't had a chance to taste-test the cake pops beforehand, like I usually did. But I wouldn't — couldn't — have put anything black and oozy in them.

My dad immediately offered everyone refunds on their pops, and girls took their money and practically ran out the door. Soon it was just me, Gwen, Tansy, and Dad left standing in shock. The remnants of crushed cake pops lay scattered and mashed into the floor, some of the jewelry had been knocked off its stands, and the whole place looked like an earthquake had struck.

"Well, I knew my jewelry was a tad on the edgy side," Gwen said, picking a pair of earrings off the floor. "But I had no idea I'd have them running and screaming."

She was trying to keep things light, as always, but disappointment tinged her face.

"Gwen, I'm so sorry," I said. "I have no idea what happened."

"But you can figure it out," Tansy said hopefully. "You can try again. Reschedule the show . . ."

"Tansy!" I said impatiently, wanting her for once to be realistic. "Nobody's going to come to another show after this. Just . . . stop, okay?"

Tansy's eyes widened in surprise. "Okay," she said softly.

"Gwendolyn, Tansy," my dad said quietly. "Go home, *por favor*. Alicia and I will clean up everything."

"But, Mr. Ramirez," Tansy started, "let us help please. . . ."

My dad shook his head. "I need to talk to Alicia now . . . alone."

And that did it. They knew a doomsayer when they heard one. My friends both gave me sympathetic looks. I wanted to follow them right out the door, because I knew what was coming, and I was dreading it.

The door jingled its way into silence, and my dad collapsed into a chair, his head in his hands.

"*Bastante*. Enough," he said. "You're done making cake pops. *No más*."

And there it was. The words I'd been dreading.

"Dad, today was a freak accident," I said, panic rising inside me. "I don't even know what went wrong, but I'll find out. I'll make it right. . . ."

"Do you have any idea what today cost us?" he asked. "We paid three hundred dollars for all of the supplies, and we had to refund everyone. The bakery's reputation will be ruined after this!"

"Don't say that. It won't be that bad. If I win the bake-off, we'll get a lot more customers. . . ."

He shook his head, sighing. "I'm not going to stop you from competing in the bake-off. I know it's important to you. But as for our bakery, I should never have let you sell cake pops here in the first place. It was a mistake. I played along with this, this silly idea, and look what happened. Disaster!"

"Silly idea?" I repeated, my voice rising into a yell. "Of course you thought it was silly! You hate *any* new idea!" I paced around the table, balling my hands into fists. "You're stuck on your prehistoric breads and pastries, and it's all because you're afraid." I sucked in a breath, but then barreled on before I could stop myself, "Ever since mom died, you've been afraid —"

I clamped my mouth shut as Dad's face paled.

"What did you say?" he whispered, his hands clutching the edge of the table.

I hesitated. I could backpedal and pretend I'd never said it, or I could finally tell him the truth and deal with the consequences.

I met his eyes. "You heard what I said, Dad. You hide in this bakery all day long. You don't talk about her. You don't even want to think about her. I know how she used to bake. Abuelita Rosa told me. Mom took risks. She tried new things. But you . . . you can't handle it." Tears were pooling in my eyes now. "You're just going to wait and watch while we go under."

My dad slammed his palm down onto the table. "I've heard enough! I've made my decision, Alicia. No more cake pops, and that's the end of the discussion."

"Fine," I sobbed. "But if you won't fight for this place, I will."

I ran into the kitchen as the tears coursed down my cheeks, and a few seconds later, I heard my dad hang up the CLOSED sign and walk out the front door. I sank down onto a stool and let the floodgates open. I couldn't believe it. In just a few hours, I'd lost my cake pops and probably the bakery, too. My dad was right. We might not recover from this fiasco, and then what would we do? What if we had to close our doors, and it was all my fault?

When I'd finally cried myself out, I wearily faced the mess I'd made. Measuring cups, bowls, and spoons lay piled up, crusted with dried batter. Slowly, I began moving everything into the sink. But when I lifted up the largest mixing bowl, something rolled off the counter and onto my shoe.

I glanced down. It was a small cooking syringe, and inside it were a few drops of black liquid. I turned it over in my hands. I hadn't been using the syringe while baking, so why was it out? I inspected the counters more carefully, and then I saw it. A bottle of black food coloring.

A horrible realization began to take hold. I hurried into the dining room, grabbed one of the uneaten cake pops, took it back into the kitchen, and sliced it open. As I did, a stream of black liquid squirted out of the morello cherry at the center. Suddenly, all the pieces fell into place, and I knew what had happened.

Someone had injected black food coloring into all of the cherries before I'd put them in the cake pops. It had to be someone who wanted to ruin the jewelry show, someone who was jealous. Or, someone who wanted to ruin my dad's business once and for all. Fiery rage swept through me as a certain face appeared in my mind. I knew who had done this, and there was no way I was going to let him get away with it.

Chapter Nine

I practically ran to school on Monday morning, and charged through the hallways on a seek-and-destroy mission. Soon enough, I found Dane, leaning against his locker casually munching on a muffin and talking with Jake. His face broke into a wide smile when he saw me, and it took everything in me not to shove that muffin right into that inflated head of his.

"Hey," Dane said brightly. "How did your show go?"

My eyes must have glowed red, because the complacent expression on his face was replaced with something like fear.

"Are you kidding me?" I snarled. "You know *exactly* how it went."

He raised his eyebrows. "What do you mean?"

"You sabotaged the whole thing!" I yelled. I was vaguely aware of a few brave onlookers hovering around us, probably enjoying the mini-drama. Jake was backing away from us uncomfortably. "You put the food coloring in the pops," I continued furiously. "You ruined everything!"

Dane's forehead wrinkled in confusion. "I don't know what you're talking about, Ali. Seriously, I —"

"You said you wanted a truce. That we were friends."

He shrugged helplessly. "I did. We are." He shook his head in frustration. "I . . . I don't even know why you're freaking out on me right now. This is crazy!"

I hesitated for a split second, studying his crestfallen face. I had to hand it to him. He really looked like he didn't have a clue. But I was not going to be duped by his innocent act.

"You want to shut down my dad's business," I seethed. "Well, it's working. No one came to the bakery this weekend. Not one person! And you didn't have the guts to play fair. You had to go behind my back and do something so . . . so jerky!" I took a step toward him and he backed into his locker, holding up his hands like he was ready to block punches. Of course, I wasn't about to punch him. But I did grab his muffin and smash it on the ground, not that it made me feel much better. And, at the same time, my book bag slipped out of my hand and crashed onto the floor along with the muffin, dumping books and papers everywhere.

"Aagh!" I cried. "*Now* look what you made me do!" I bent down, hurriedly shoving my now crumb-covered books back into my bag. The adrenaline that had been fueling my tirade was nearly out, and the threat of tears was closing in.

"Here," Dane said, bending down, "let me help you clean it up."

I pushed away his hands. "No! I don't need your help." My eyes were burning from holding back tears. "Just . . . leave me alone!"

I grabbed the last of my papers and pushed past the crowd of watching kids, making it to the bathroom just in time for the waterworks to erupt.

I locked myself into a stall and collapsed on the toilet seat, letting all the disappointment of the last few days crash over me. When I heard the bathroom door creak open, I sniffled back a sob, hoping whoever it was would be in and out quickly. No such luck. Two seconds later there was a sharp rap on the stall door.

"I just caught wind of someone having a breakdown in front of half the school," a familiar voice said. "Long dark hair, hazel eyes, has a quirky baking fetish. You haven't seen her around, have you?"

"Go away, Gwen." I tried to say it firmly, but it sounded like a pathetic kitten mewling. "You don't want to be around me right now. I have an acute case of loser-itis coming on. It might be contagious."

Gwen laughed. "I'll take my chances. You have a test in world science tomorrow, remember? You know you won't be able to live with yourself if you don't show your face in class. What if you miss something that shows up on the test? The bell's about to ring. Come on, open up."

I glared at the stall door. Gwen was tapping into my weakness and she knew it. Even though I'd already been over my handmade flash cards for the world science test, if I missed some key factoid by skipping class I'd be crushed. I sighed, dragged myself off the toilet seat, and unlocked the door.

Gwen grimaced. "Cripes, you're an ugly crier."

I giggled as she yanked me out of the stall and started dabbing my face with paper towels.

"I can't believe he wouldn't even admit what he did," I said. "And now I have to sit next to him in world science!"

"Don't talk to him. Don't look at him," Gwen said. "Just get through class and get out of there. We'll talk more at lunch, okay?"

I nodded and hugged her. "Thanks," I said. "I can't believe you're not more upset. It was *your* show he ruined."

Gwen patted my hair into place. "There'll be other shows. And I plan on having them at Say It With Flour. So it better not go anywhere, right?"

I smiled. "Right."

The bell rang, and Gwen walked me to class, promising to take out Dane if he came within ten feet of me for the rest of the day. But he didn't. In fact, when I got to world science, I found him sitting in the last row, a dozen seats away from me. I guessed he'd asked Mr. Jenkins to change his seat, and I breathed a sigh of relief. At least I didn't have to deal with the awkwardness of sitting next to him. Hopefully the rest of the day might go more smoothly.

I was wrong.

When I got to the quad for lunch, kids walking by me mumbled under their breaths and gave me sideways glances of sympathy, disbelief, or even disgust.

"I guess the whole school knows about what happened on Saturday," I said as I sat down with Gwen and Tansy.

"Who cares?" Gwen said. Then she snickered. "I don't even care that I didn't sell more jewelry. Seeing black goo oozing from Lissie and Jane's mouths was completely worth it."

"Shh," I hissed, elbowing Gwen as Sarah walked over, her lips pursed unpleasantly.

"Sarah," I started, hoping that if I took the initiative she'd be more understanding. "I'm sorry about what happened on Saturday."

She sighed. "Me, too. My girls are so upset." She nodded toward where Lissie and Jane sat with their heads bent low over their table. "That black stuff still hasn't come off their teeth all the way. They're so embarrassed. They're not talking at all until it's gone."

"That's such a shame," Gwen said.

"I know," Sarah said. If she'd heard Gwen's sarcastic undertone, she didn't show it. "Well, Ali, I just wanted to let you know that I'm willing to forget the whole incident. As my father likes to say, everyone deserves a second chance. So you're still invited to be a contestant in the bake-off, no hard feelings."

"Thanks," I said, trying to make my voice convey a gratefulness I didn't feel. "I'm looking forward to it."

Sarah smiled sweetly. "Great!" she said, and bounced away.

"At least she's not mad," Tansy said.

"Maybe not," I said, "but I get the feeling that this bake-off is my last chance to prove myself to Sarah. To everyone." I picked up my school bag and started rummaging through it.

"What are you doing?" Gwen asked.

"I have to win the bake-off," I said. "Maybe I can memorize some of my mom's recipes beforehand. With any luck, Sarah will pick ingredients that I can use to make one of her recipes. Sarah would never know."

"But, Ali," Tansy said quietly, "that's kind of cheating."

"Not really," I said, my stomach knotting at the word. "I'd just be . . . hedging my bets. Besides, I don't care how I do it, I have to win."

"You do care," Tansy said. "And you can win the fair way. I know you can. You just have to keep trying and everything will be okay."

"No it won't!" I cried. "Nothing I've tried to make without a recipe has been edible. So if I want to use one of my mom's recipes, then that's what I'm going to do." I reached into my bag for the recipe book, but it wasn't in its usual place. "And I'm tired of you getting all psycho cheerleader on me every time I mess up. It does *not* make me feel better, and it will *not* make everything okay!"

Tansy blinked at me, stunned. "I . . . I didn't know you felt that way," she said, her lip quivering. "I didn't mean to —"

"Just forget it." I sighed. Her hurt expression was making the knot in my stomach even bigger, and I couldn't meet her eyes anymore. They were starting to fill with tears.

She stood up quickly. "I just remembered that I have a library book I have to return." Her voice broke. "I'll see you guys later."

"Whoa, Ali," Gwen said quietly. "A little harsh, don't you think?"

I felt a stab of guilt. I thought about hurrying after Tansy to apologize, but I was too busy digging into my bag, and still coming up empty-handed. Now my guilt was shifting into panic.

"I know my mom's book was in here. Where *is* it?"

Then, with a sudden sinking feeling, I knew. I closed my eyes and gripped the edge of my seat. "Oh no. It must have fallen out when I dropped my bag in the hallway this morning. I have to find it." I stood up and started toward the lockers.

"Wait!" Gwen called. "I'll come with you."

"No, it's okay," I said, taking off at a jog. "I'll catch up with you in a few minutes."

But a few minutes turned into twenty. I scoured the hallway, looking all around Dane's locker, mine, the bathroom. Finally, when I only had a few minutes before the lunch bell rang, I went to the office to check the lost and found. It wasn't there, either. The book had disappeared.

The bell rang, and I was still standing helplessly outside the office, not knowing where else to look and feeling tears threatening all over again. Then I felt a hand on my shoulder, and turned to see Harris, worry in his eyes.

"Are you okay?" he asked. "You look pretty upset."

"Just a killer day, that's all," I said.

"Yeah, Gwen told me what happened at the jewelry show. What a bummer. I'm really sorry."

"Me, too," I said. "But I'll figure things out. I think."

"I know you will, Ali. You're not the kind of girl who gives up easily." He smiled. "So . . . there's this thing I've been wanting to talk to you about. . . ."

I closed my eyes, the pit in my stomach opening up into a black hole. *Oh no.* It was happening again. Harris was going to ask me out, and if he did that right now, when everything was falling apart, I would so not be able to deal. *Not now. Please not now.*

I cracked one eye open a slit, and saw him checking his watch. "You know what? We'll have to talk later. If I'm late to Mrs. Waters's class again, she'll tell Coach Tom, and he'll bench me. Are you sure you're okay?"

"Absolutely," I lied, and gave him a weak smile as he waved and walked away.

But the second he was out of sight, I slumped against the wall, knowing nothing would be okay until I found my mom's book. And right now, the chances of that happening were looking pretty grim.

That afternoon I walked by the bakery and kept right on going. I couldn't stand seeing my dad's worry-lined face and a dining room full of empty tables. Instead, I walked home. It was a beautiful sunshiny day, but I didn't notice the blooming geraniums or pungent eucalyptus trees. All I could see was my mom's missing book in my mind.

When Gwen walked into my house two hours later with Abuelita Rosa and Roberto, the three of them found me drowning my sorrows in a fudge brownie. My third.

"Whoa." Gwen braced herself against the kitchen door frame, clutching her chest. "Don't tell me you're actually eating a brownie from a box?"

"Yup," I said, taking another big bite. "I've hit rock bottom."

"I'll say," she said, plunking down in the chair across from me. "I never thought you'd stoop so low. You're way better than a store-bought mix."

"No." I shook my head vehemently. "This is my future. A life of prepackaged ingredients."

Roberto scrambled onto my lap and grabbed the remains of my brownie.

"Yum," he said as he gobbled. "Prepackaged brownies are pretty good!"

Abuelita Rosa kissed my cheek and slid a glass of milk toward me. "*¿Qué pasó, niñita?* You didn't come to the bakery after school today. We got worried."

"Yeah, and Harris kicked my butt at *Dragonlore*," Gwen said. "I really could've used some moral support."

I stared at the table. "I can't find Mom's recipe book," I said in a trembling voice. "I looked everywhere. I even thought I might have left it at home. But I checked my room. It's gone." I looked hesitantly at Abuelita, afraid she was going to be furious. After all, my mom was her only daughter, and the book was probably as precious to her as it was to me. But she only smiled at me patiently.

"It's probably somewhere you never thought to look," she said calmly. "So stop trying to find it and let *it* find you."

I shook my head. "I don't understand why all these awful things keep happening. The jewelry show was a disaster. I was a complete beast to Tansy today, and she's never been anything but sweet to me! I tried to catch her alone in phys ed to apologize, but she totally avoided me. And now Mom's book is gone!" I tried not to burst into tears.

Gwen gave me a level look. "Your mom's book will turn up. You can make up with Tansy. And you can still turn things around at the bakery," she said. "You have another chance to prove yourself at the bake-off. If you win, you'll be guaranteed one big piece of business."

"That's the other thing." I groaned. "The bake-off is in two weeks and I'm not ready." I put my head in my hands. "Maybe I should drop out."

Gwen's eyes hit saucer status. "Are you kidding? And let Dane win after what he did to you? No way!"

"Well, I'll never win anyway." I dabbed at some brownie crumbs with my finger and popped them into my mouth. "I try so hard, and nothing ever works the way it's supposed to."

"You've been trying *too* hard," Abuelita said. "Following the rules doesn't guarantee perfection. You have to leave room for some serendipity." She squeezed my hand. "Stop trying to make things perfect. Instead, try to make them perfectly *you*."

"Perfectly me," I whispered. Fear formed a cold lump in my stomach. I looked from Abuelita to Gwen, my eyes filling. "What if . . . what if I don't know what that is?"

"Great," Gwen said. "*Now* you're having an identity crisis?" She shook my shoulders. "This is no time for soul searching. Stare in the mirror for fifteen minutes, and get a grip!"

I gawked at Gwen, and then we all broke into giggles.

"I'm just saying, enough with the self-pity," Gwen said when we'd quieted down. "It's time to get your caboose into the kitchen to do some work."

I dried my eyes and took a deep breath, looking around the table at these people who loved me. These people who believed in me way more than they should have. "Okay," I said.

"*¡Fantástico!*" Abuelita clapped her hands. "And no matter what happens, you'll have the satisfaction of knowing you tried." Then she hugged me and took Roberto into the family room to read some books before dinner.

Tried. I thought about that word. It was a word people meant as encouraging, but really they used it when they were prepping you for failure. Well, trying wasn't good enough for me. "I have to beat Dane at the bake-off," I said to Gwen. "There's no other option."

"That's it," Gwen said. "Focus on sweet revenge."

I stood and picked up the remaining brownies. "Ugh. I can't believe I ate these." I was about to tip them into the trash when Gwen grabbed them.

"Hang on a sec!" she said. "I said *you* shouldn't stoop to pre-packaged treats. I never said *I* shouldn't." She bit into one and grinned.

Later that evening, I tried to focus on homework, but my mind kept racing in circles around the bake-off, Harris, my mom's missing book, my fight with Tansy, and Dane. And then I zeroed in on Dane. Dane, Dane, Dane. Maybe this whole thing wasn't my fault as much as it was his. His fault that the jewelry show got ruined; his fault that I lost my mom's book; his fault that my dad's business was losing money.

But he wasn't going to stop me from winning the bake-off. And when I won, Dane would realize that all his sly tricks and smooth-talking amounted to nothing. I tried to tell myself that it would feel terrific to topple Dane right off his Perk Up pedestal. But maybe Gwen had gotten revenge all wrong. Because, if the knot twisting inside me was any indication, revenge wasn't sweet at all. It was bitter, sour, and hard to stomach.

Chapter Ten

When I walked into Say It With Flour on Friday after school, the last thing I expected to see was my dad waving me into his back office — the office he never used except when he was doing inventory or paying taxes. I'd been tiptoeing around him since our fight after the jewelry show, and we'd barely spoken to each other for most of the week.

"What's up?" I whispered to Abuelita Rosa as I walked past the booth where she and Roberto were playing Go Fish.

She looked up at me, and when I saw the sadness in her eyes,

I knew. Something awful was coming. She sighed and patted my arm. "I'll let your father tell you."

I'd been worried before, but now I was terrified. The week had been a disaster already. Tansy had started eating lunch with her dance-team friends instead of with me and Gwen, and she went out of her way to avoid me. And who could blame her? I'd been awful to her. My mom's recipe book was still missing, Say It With Flour was still a ghost town, and I hadn't baked one thing that worked without a recipe. I only had one week left. If I didn't figure this out, not only was I going to lose to Dane, but I was going to look like a complete idiot doing it. What else could possibly go wrong?

I walked through the kitchen to the tiny pantry at the back that my dad had long ago converted to his office. He sat with his head hanging low over his accounting ledger — a handwritten book he still insisted on keeping even though he knew perfectly well how to use the accounting program on his computer. His shoulders were sinking inward and his mouth was drawn taut as a tightrope.

"Dad?" I said quietly. "What's the matter?"

He lifted his eyes from his ledger to my face, and I was shocked to see how old he suddenly looked, so old and so tired.

"I've made a decision about the bakery," he said slowly. "You're not going to like it. . . ."

My breath caught in my throat and my knees wobbled. I wanted to cover my ears, or run out the door so that I wouldn't hear the words that had to be coming.

"We're going to close the shop at the end of the month," he said. "We've been losing too much money." He sighed. "I've already taken more money out of our savings than I wanted to, just to pay the rent and keep us going. I can't anymore."

"No, Dad, you can," I pleaded. "Things will get better. If I win the bake-off, we'll get our business back, plus more."

He smiled forlornly. "Alicia, I told you that you can do your bake-off, and that's fine. If you win, we'll cater Sarah's party, but then we're done. I'm not going to change my mind."

"Please, Dad, take some time to think about it. We can bake less, cut costs, something!" My voice was shaking. I had to convince my dad he was making a huge mistake.

He stood up slowly, like this whole discussion was taking every ounce of energy he had in him. "You were right, you know, when you said I was afraid to take chances." He stared at the floor. "I'm sorry. I should've done more with the business a long time ago. I should've worked to grow it, try new things. Before Perk Up came along."

"We still can," I said. "It's not too late."

My dad studied me, and for a split second I saw a faint spark in his eyes. But just as quickly, it blinked out. "Sometimes I think that your mom took all of my courage with her when she left us," he said softly. "I'm tired of fighting this battle all the time, of struggling to break even. I love this bakery, but I'm going to have to let it go." He pressed his hand to my cheek. "And so will you, *hijita*."

"You're wrong, Dad," I said. "Mom didn't take all of your courage. It takes courage to raise a son and daughter alone. It takes courage to fight for the things you love." I wrapped my arms around him tight, pressing my face into his shirt collar. "I was wrong to say those things about you. I'm sorry."

He brushed my hair back from my face. *"Está bien.* It's all right. I'm just sorry I'm disappointing you. I know how much Say It With Flour means to you." He blew out a weary breath. "I think I'll go help Roberto. There won't be any customers today, and your grandmother plays a mean Go Fish."

He gave me a small smile and stepped through the door, leaving me alone.

"I'm not giving up yet," I whispered. "And you shouldn't, either."

My dad, of course, was right. Not one customer walked through the doors the rest of the day, and finally, as if he was trying to get used to the idea, my dad decided to close up early. I'd been doing my homework at one of the tables, but I put it away and offered to finish cleaning up for him. I could tell he didn't have the heart to do it.

He seemed relieved to go, as if he was worried that the bakery was angry at being abandoned. I could sense it, too. There was a loneliness settling over the store, like the walls had heard us talking about closing, and they understood.

I was turning the last of the chairs over onto the tables so that I could mop, when the front bell jingled. I glanced up, wondering who was actually brave enough (or foolish enough) to set foot in our accursed shop.

And I came face-to-face with Dane.

"We're closed," I said, feeling fury roiling up inside me. He had some nerve coming in here.

"Really?" Dane challenged, nodding toward the front window. "The sign still says 'open.'"

Grrr. Now I was even angrier. "Do you always have to prove your point?"

"I don't know." He stared me down. "Do you always have to jump to conclusions?"

"I don't know what you're talking about." I glowered, crossing my arms.

"You will in about ten seconds," he said, swinging his backpack onto the bench of one of the booths. "And then you're going to feel really guilty." He reached into his backpack and pulled something out.

I gasped. It was my mom's recipe book.

"Where did you find this?" I demanded, taking it and hugging it to my chest. "I looked all over school."

"You forgot to pick it up," Dane said. "On Monday when you spilled your books by my locker. I saw it afterward, but you were so mad at me, I was afraid you'd punch me or something if I tried to give it back."

"I wouldn't have," I said. But then again, maybe I would've. I turned the book over in my hands, a reluctant thank-you on the tip of my tongue. But then my eyes narrowed. "Wait a second, you held on to this book all week long. Why?" I clutched the book tighter. "Did you read it? Are you going to steal my recipes now, too?"

Dane held up his hands. "Whoa, hang on —"

I whirled away from him. "Of course you'd do that. To make sure Perk Up keeps the upper hand. I can't believe you!"

"Ali!" He grabbed my shoulders and turned me toward him. "Would you just listen to me for a minute?" His face reddened with frustration, and I squirmed a little, but he didn't let me go. "You always assume the worst about me, and honestly, I'm getting sick of it."

"Well, why should I trust you? You ruined the jewelry show with that little food-dye trick of yours, and now you show up with my book after keeping it all week? What am I supposed to think?"

Dane frowned. "For starters, *if* we were friends, I could tell you that it wasn't me that put that food coloring in your cake pops. And, *if* we were friends, you'd believe me. But I guess my first mistake was in thinking we were ever friends in the first place, right?"

"Right," I blurted without thinking. "I mean, wrong." I stomped my foot. "I mean, I don't know!"

"At least I got you to admit that much," he said.

I shook loose of his grasp and glared at him. "Okay," I said reluctantly. "I'm listening."

Dane brushed a hand through his thick hair. "No, I did *not* ruin your cake pops. I swear it. I don't know who did it, or why. But remember Sarah and Lissie were both in your kitchen that day, too."

"True." I faltered. I hadn't thought about that before. "But Lissie ate one of the pops. And Sarah . . . why would Sarah do that to her own friends?"

Dane shrugged. "Who knows? Maybe you should ask her."

"No way," I said quickly. "What if I was wrong? I don't want to get on Sarah's bad side . . . ever. Mayor Chan could probably shut down Say It With Flour in a heartbeat, if he wanted to."

"Okay," Dane said. "It's your call. But you have to trust me that I had nothing to do with it."

I studied his face, trying to detect any sign of lying. But all I saw was a blatant, challenging look of honesty. The truth was, as angry as I was at him, a small part of me wanted desperately to believe that maybe he really was innocent.

"I'd like to believe that," I said finally. "I really would."

"Okay," he said. "And yes, I looked through your book. But not because I was stealing recipes. I would never do that." He sighed, staring at me with piercing eyes. "I wish you understood that about me." He paused, seeming to think over his next words carefully. "I looked through the book because I was curious about . . . about you."

"Oh," I barely squeaked out. He tried to hold my gaze, but I dropped my eyes, embarrassment flooding through me.

"But they're not your recipes, are they?" he asked quietly. "I take French, not Spanish, so I couldn't translate, but I thought the book had the name Estrella in it?"

I nodded. "It was my mom's recipe book. Her name was Estrella. I've been using her recipes to make my cake pops for the store."

"They're good recipes," he said. "Really different."

"Yours are, too," I said. "It seems like I'm the only one who can't . . ." I let my voice die, catching myself just in time.

Dane raised his eyebrows. "Can't what?"

I hesitated, knowing this was a testing point between us. If I truly believed Dane was innocent, I could come clean and confess my secret. If I didn't believe him, there was no way I was going to give him more ammunition to use against me. I closed my eyes and a voice deep inside me said, *Trust him.* So I did.

I took a deep breath and blurted, "I can't bake without using other people's recipes. I can't make up my own. I've tried . . . *so* many times. It doesn't work for me."

"Wow." Dane whistled under his breath. "*That* could be a little problem at the bake-off."

I shot him a dirty look. "This is not a time for jokes."

"So . . . what are you going to do?"

"Not back out, if that's what you're hoping for."

"I'm not." He rolled his eyes. "In fact, I was hoping to have to fight for a win." He took a step toward the kitchen. "So I guess we'd better get started."

"With what?" I asked. "Where are you going?"

"I'm going to the kitchen." He grinned. "You're going to bake. Right here. Right now. No recipes."

"With you?" I shook my head. "I don't think so."

Dane smirked. "Look, I don't have any actual proof that I'm a nice guy. But I am trying to help you. If you don't believe that, then *you're* not as smart or as nice as I thought you were." With that, he walked into the kitchen.

I stood by the counter, glaring after him. How was it possible to be so aggravated, flustered, and flattered all at once? The pride in me wanted to make him sweat it for a while, but my curiosity (and yes, desperation) won out, and I followed him into the kitchen.

It must not have occurred to him that I'd say no, because he was already setting out various sized bowls and pouring flour, sugar, and baking soda into them. He pulled a jumble of spices and extracts from the pantry and some eggs from the fridge.

"Now point me in the direction of the music," he said.

I motioned to the shop's stereo, and Dane pulled his iPod out of his back pocket and slid it into the docking station. A smooth, jaunty trumpet and saxophone filled the kitchen.

"Jazz?" I asked.

He smiled. "New Orleans jazz. I can't bake without it." He grabbed a hand towel and started toward me. "Now I have to do one more thing. . . ."

He spun me around, and before I'd barely gotten a protest out, he'd tied the towel around my head, blindfolding me.

"I'm supposed to bake without seeing the ingredients?" I asked, incredulous.

"Your other senses will take over," he said. "You'll see."

He took my hand in his warm one, and led me over to the counter. "Okay, let your fingers find their way."

I gave a skeptical laugh, but I reached my free hand out. I cautiously dipped my hand into a bowl and touched satiny powder.

"Flour?" I guessed.

"You got it," Dane said.

I kept going, and soon I'd identified all the ingredients except the spices.

"For those," Dane said. "You need to smell, or taste."

I did, and managed to get all of them right.

"See, your body knows more than your mind thinks it does," he said. "So now start playing. Don't think about how it will turn out. Just have fun with the process."

"But how do I measure?" I asked. "I need my measuring spoons and cups."

"Nope." His voice came from by my shoulder. "Do it by feel. Try to feel the weight of things. Then taste as you go."

I hesitated, every fiber of me wanting to take off the blindfold and give up. My fingers itched to hold my measuring spoons, to know with certainty how much I was adding. But after a minute,

I scooped up some flour, felt the weight of it in my hand, and tried to gauge the amount. Then I added sugar, and from there, my fingers began to move smoothly, almost magically, blending mystery ingredients until I had a bowl full of batter that tasted amazing.

"All done," Dane said, lifting the blindfold so that I could survey my work. He pointed to the bowl. "If I were in New Orleans, I'd call it cake-pop gumbo."

"I call it a mess," I said, surveying the gelatinous glob, and the broken egg shells and mounds of spilled baking soda and sugar all over the counter. "How many times have you baked like this before?"

"Um . . . never." He laughed at my shocked face. "But I thought it might work for you."

I poured the batter into a cake pan and popped it into the oven. While my mysterious mixture was baking, Dane and I cleaned up. I was amazed at how easily we fell into talking, just like we had on the day of the whale-watching trip. In fact, I actually felt a pang of disappointment when the timer beeped, interrupting us.

I slid out my cake, marveling at its perfectly golden crusted top. It smelled delicious. I carefully cut myself a slice and when I took a bite, I discovered that it tasted even better than it smelled.

"I can't believe it," I cried, an ecstatic grin growing on my face. "It worked!"

Dane leaned back against the counter, looking very pleased with himself. "I knew it would."

I raised my eyebrows. "You did not."

He shrugged and laughed. "Okay, I *hoped* it would. Besides, it was all you. I can't take any credit."

"Thank you," I said. I ducked my head, feeling sheepish. "You know, I never really gave you a fair chance before tonight. I'm . . . I'm sorry for that. Normally, I'm not so tough on people. But for some reason, you're different."

"You mean I'm a pain in the butt," he said with a grin. "Point taken."

"No," I said. "You're not. You're not anything like I thought you were at all."

I felt myself blush as the words left my mouth. Was it my imagination or was Dane blushing, too?

He shuffled his feet and pushed his blond hair out his eyes. "Um . . . thanks. I think." He checked his watch. "It's late, and I have a cross-country meet first thing in the morning. I better go."

I nodded, and we walked to the front of the shop.

"See you at school on Monday," I said, suddenly feeling lighter about everything. Even the fate of the bakery and my fight with Tansy.

"See you," Dane echoed. Then he stopped, meeting my gaze. "And, you know, you should keep practicing. I want you to make me sweat at the bake-off next Saturday."

"I'll give it my best shot," I said.

"You just have to trust yourself. And . . ." He stepped closer, until our faces were only inches apart. "Make sure you get the batter in the bowl. Not on your face." He gently wiped at a spot on my cheek while my face caught fire.

Our eyes met, and for one crazy minute I thought he might be about to kiss me. For one crazy minute, I thought that I might want him to. But he didn't. He pulled away and went through the door, waving good-bye.

I watched him take off at a jog under the yellow streetlights, and I let out the breath I'd been holding. My heart was racing, and I could still feel a warmth in the air around me where he'd been standing. What had just happened? I wasn't sure.

But now that my own guard was down, I could see that what I'd always thought of as arrogance in Dane was more a defense mechanism. Underneath, he was sweet, funny, and kind.

And as I locked up the store and walked home under a crystal clear sky strewn with stars, he was all I could think about.

Chapter Eleven

The sea of green and yellow T-shirts swarmed before my eyes like something out of a nightmare, and my first instinct was to turn around and go straight back home.

It was the Friday morning before the bake-off, and I'd woken up thinking I was ready. That was until I got to school. Now I watched in a bewildered fog as Lissie and Jane walked by wearing matching green T-shirts that read TEAM DANE.

"Hey, Ali," Lissie said with the fakest attempt at an apologetic grin I'd ever seen. "Just getting into the bake-off spirit. No offense."

I nodded mutely, trying to process what she meant. But then Gwen was at my side, leading me toward the quad.

"You are not going to believe this," Gwen hissed in my ear. Sarah stood in the center of the quad, surrounded by open boxes, pulling out T-shirts and handing them to every kid who walked by.

I saw Tyler and Angie from my English class yanking yellow TEAM ALICIA shirts over their normal clothes, and other kids holding one shirt of each color, trying to pick a team.

"Oh my god," I mumbled. "She's pitting me against Dane in front of the entire student body. . . ." The twinge of nerves I'd felt about the bake-off suddenly grew into a wracking earthquake. "I am not going to survive this."

"Sure you are," Gwen said. "You've been baking nonstop for the last week. Without Renata or recipes. And your cake pops are genius. You're ready."

I had to admit Gwen was right. Every time I'd been tempted to reach for my measuring spoons, I'd thought about baking with Dane, how the right mixture of ingredients felt and tasted.

And I'd finally hit my stride. But now I felt insecure all over again.

Gwen grabbed three TEAM ALICIA shirts.

"Who's the extra for?" I asked.

"The MIA musketeer, of course," Gwen said. She jerked her head toward the lockers, and I saw Tansy, focusing on her combination lock and trying hard not to look in our direction.

"She's not going to be there tomorrow," I sighed, my stomach sinking. "She hasn't returned any of my calls or texts. She hates me. And I don't blame her."

"She does not," Gwen said. "I've been talking to her. She just doesn't want to get yelled at again. But she loves you. She'll be there tomorrow. You'll see." Gwen held up the T-shirts. "Well, we might as well suit up." When I gave her a skeptical look, she held up her finger to quiet me. Then she grabbed a black marker out of her bag and wrote in huge bubble letters on the back of each shirt: SAY IT WITH FLOUR.

"There," she said proudly. "Now it's not all tackiness. It's advertising." She held up her marker like a sword. "I'm going to go see how many shirts I can 'fix' before the bell." Then she dashed off down the hallway.

I giggled and pulled my shirt over my head. When I looked up, Dane was riding his bike slowly up to the edge of the crowd, taking in the chaos. He barely had time to stop his bike before Sarah pranced over to him.

"Dane!" She gave him a sweet smile and held a TEAM DANE tee up under his chin. "There! I *knew* I'd picked the right shade of green. It matches your eyes perfectly!"

Dane looked like he was trying not to laugh. "Thanks," he said, and then started to shove the shirt into his backpack.

Sarah's smile faltered. "Aren't you going to put it on?"

He hesitated and glanced up. Our eyes met for a second, and my heart skittered. He grinned at me and rolled his eyes in Sarah's direction, and I felt like our thoughts were completely in tune. That Dane thought the whole thing was just as ridiculous as I did.

As I was about to smile back, Harris stepped in front of me, beaming.

"Ali!" He motioned to his yellow shirt. "Gwen just doctored up my shirt. Better, right?"

I gave a start, realizing that Harris didn't have nearly the same effect on me that Dane did. What did that mean?

"Thanks, Harris," I said. "It's nice of you to wear it, but you don't have to."

"Of course I do. Friends always get each other's backs, right?" He leaned toward me. "Besides, I'm actually scared of what Gwen might do to me if I *don't* wear it."

I laughed. "I don't blame you."

"The whole soccer team's going to be there tomorrow after our game to root for you," he said as he swung his backpack over his shoulder. "You'll win, hands down."

"We'll see," I called after him.

Once he was gone, I looked back toward Dane and spotted him chatting with Sarah. She'd worked her magic and gotten him to put on the shirt. And she'd been right; it did match the color of his eyes exactly.

I watched them as they talked, smiling at each other. Jealousy gnawed at me, but I told myself to stop being silly.

Yes, Dane and I had talked before world science almost every day since he'd stopped by the bakery, and the tension between us had eased. We hadn't argued once, and I found myself looking forward to seeing him in class. More often than I liked to admit, I also thought about that strange, confusing moment with him when I'd sensed we might've kissed, but didn't. I replayed it in my head, wondering if I'd imagined it, or if it'd been real.

Now, as I watched him talk with Sarah, I told myself I must've imagined it. After all, he was almost as close to Sarah now as he'd been to me on Friday night. If he moved a few inches, their lips would touch. And the way Sarah was flirting with him, maybe that's what she wanted.

The bell rang, and I forced myself to look away, to make my feet move toward class. I reminded myself that tomorrow morning, once again, Dane and I would be rivals. I couldn't be thinking about a completely imagined near kiss when I needed to be thinking about winning the bake-off and saving Say It With Flour.

If I won the bake-off, maybe my dad would at least consider keeping the bakery open. I didn't want to lose Dane's friendship, but I *couldn't* lose Say It With Flour. So come tomorrow, the bake-off was all that mattered.

<hr />

After a restless night of dreams that involved tidal waves of cake pops crashing over me, I stumbled into our kitchen on Saturday morning. I was so bleary-eyed that I nearly missed my dad, who was sitting at the table, nibbling on a *concha*.

"Why aren't you at the bakery?" I asked, sitting down beside him.

He took a sip of his coffee. "Oh, I decided to open an hour later today. I wanted to be here to wish you luck at the bake-off. Besides, I was looking through this. . . ." He patted an open book in front of him.

I blinked, and then my eyes widened, adrenaline surging through me. It was Mom's recipe book.

"Where did you get that?" I whispered.

"You left it on your nightstand," my dad said. "I was putting away laundry yesterday and saw it."

"Oh." *Stupid me!* How could I have left it out for him to find? I held my breath and risked a glance at my dad, wondering how mad he was going to be. To my surprise, though, he didn't look angry at all. Instead, he had a soft, sad smile on his face.

"No te preocupes." His voice was quiet, gentle. "Don't worry. I'm not mad. Your abuelita explained everything." He met my eyes, his own glazed with tears. "It's right that you should have it. I'm glad . . . very glad . . . that she saved it."

"You are?" I couldn't hide the surprise in my voice.

He nodded, running his fingers across the pages. "Of course. It was wrong of me to give away so many of your mom's things. I didn't think that you might need them later, when you got older." He sighed. "When your heart is broken, sometimes your mind does things that don't make much sense. I'm sorry."

"It's okay," I whispered. "At least we still have it."

"Yes," he said. "So this is what you were using to make your cake pops for the shop?"

I nodded. "I should've told you," I said quietly. "But I was afraid you'd take the book away."

"I thought I recognized some of those recipes you used," he admitted. Then he smiled again, this time happily. He reached for my hands, taking them in his own. "You have your mother's hands. She used to say that her hands were the best measuring cups in the world. That was the only way she baked, with her hands."

"I didn't know that." I could almost see her in the bakery, scooping up flour and sugar, letting it sift through her fingers until the weight of it felt just right.

"I wish I could've done right by her," Dad said, looking down. "She wanted you and Roberto to run the bakery someday with your families. But now that's just not possible."

I nearly opened my mouth to argue, but then thought better of it. There was no point in getting into another fight with Dad about the bakery now, especially when I hadn't won or lost the bake-off yet.

He patted my hands. "She'd be so proud of you, Alicia, with what you've done with your cake pops and now competing in this bake-off. She'd be so happy to know that you have her special talent, too."

"Thanks, Dad," I said, blinking back tears. "But I don't know about this bake-off. Dane's an amazing baker. I'm not sure I can compete with him."

My father's eyes locked on my face, unwavering. "You can," he said simply, as if it weren't even a question. "You will." He pulled me into a firm hug, and I stayed there longer than I had since I was small, hoping he was right. Hoping that maybe, somewhere inside me, some piece of my mother lived to give me the courage I needed to get through this day.

I'd known that Sarah had whipped the kids at school up into a mild frenzy over the bake-off. I'd expected that maybe fifty or so kids would show up in their team tees to watch Dane and I compete.

What I didn't expect was a mob.

As Abuelita Rosa turned her car into the parking lot of Oak Canyon Community Park, my stomach seized. The lot was filled to overflowing, and the park itself was packed with hundreds of people. Our school band was in full uniform in the gazebo, playing "How Sweet It Is." Swarms of kids and adults stood and sat on the grass, some picnicking, some chatting, but *all* wearing team T-shirts. This was more than the entire student body at OCMS. This was more like the entire town of Oak Canyon.

The crowd was gathered around a large stage, where two baking stations had been set up, complete with ovens, work counters, and all the baking supplies anyone could possibly need. To my utter terror, there also seemed to be some sort of local news cameras setting up.

"Dios mío." Abuelita whistled under her breath. "You're going to have a bigger audience than Renata DeLuca's."

I groaned and clutched the car door handle. "That isn't what I needed to hear."

She gave my shoulder an encouraging squeeze and then got out of the car. "Roberto and I are going to find seats. Good luck. *Buena suerte.*"

Roberto high-fived me. *"Buena* sweater, Ali! Save a cake pop for me!"

I smiled at him. "I will, kiddo." *If I survive.*

I took a deep breath and then worked my way through the crowd, finally spotting Gwen and Tansy standing with Harris and his teammates by one of the large oaks. I waved at Tansy, feeling a surge of relief that she'd come. I had left her one last voice mail this morning, apologizing and asking her if she'd ever forgive me.

Now, instead of stampeding toward me all smiles, like she normally would've done, Tansy hung back, hesitating. Guilt twisted my insides, and I knew that there was no way I could focus on the bake-off with this awkwardness still between us.

"Hi," I said, motioning her over to a spot on the grass away from the others.

"Hey," she mumbled, fidgeting with the hem of her shirt. "I got your message. Message*s*. I'm sorry I didn't call back. I just haven't felt ready. . . ."

"No." I stepped forward, a lump in my throat. "*I'm* sorry, Tansy. I'm sorry I blew up at you. That was completely uncool. Everything was going wrong all at once, and I just . . . lost it."

Tansy shook her head. "I had no idea I was acting like a, a . . . psycho cheerleader, or whatever. I was just trying to help."

"I don't even know why I said that. It was horrible!" I put a hand on her arm. "You have a great way of looking at things, Tansy. If it weren't for you, Gwen would probably be a scary Goth, and I'd probably never had the guts to suggest a bake-off to Sarah in the first place. Don't ever change, okay?"

She smiled shyly. "I don't think I could anyway."

"Good." I reached out and gave her a huge hug, my spirits lifting. "I love you the way you are."

"Same here," Tansy said, hugging me back. "Even when you're a serious stress case."

We laughed together just as Gwen and Harris came up to join us. Gwen looked immensely relieved that Tansy and I had patched things up.

"Are you ready?" Gwen asked. She hugged me, then whispered in my ear, "A little tip: If you're going to throw up, do it *before* you take the stage."

"Very helpful, thanks," I said, pulling back from her and rolling my eyes at Tansy. "So Sarah alerted the news?" I asked, motioning to the cameras.

"If she didn't, Mayor Chan did," Harris said. "Apparently, he's going to give a speech about the new mall. I guess he thought he'd get a better turnout if he tied it into the bake-off."

"And . . . guess who else is here?" Tansy whispered, her dark eyes shining. "Some people from Renata DeLuca's show! There's their truck right over there!"

I followed her gaze and saw a red truck with the words THE BAKING GURU emblazoned in gold on the side. My mouth fell open as I stared.

"Is *she* here?" I whispered.

"No," Gwen said, "but I asked Lissie and Jane earlier, and it turns out that Mayor Chan's office sent an e-mail to her show. And Renata sent some scouts to check out the competition." She smiled at me. "I guess she wants to see if you and Dane are some kind of baking geniuses. If you win, maybe she'll name-drop you on the show. Who knows?"

I started trembling. "What — I — no!" I stammered. "I can't bake in front of Renata's staff! I'm not worthy!"

Gwen scoffed. "Her so-called staff are probably college interns who don't know a thing about baking. Trust me, you're worthy."

"Ali, you better get over there," Harris said. "It looks like Sarah wants to get started."

I glanced at the stage and saw Sarah and her dad standing at the microphone, beaming picture-perfect smiles. Meanwhile, I felt like I'd swallowed a roller coaster.

"Good luck," Tansy and Gwen said together, giving me a group hug. Just having Tansy back in our trio again gave me some comfort despite my nerves.

Then Harris took a step toward me. The next thing I knew, he was hugging me, too.

"Good luck," he said. I didn't want to pull away and hurt his feelings, but I didn't want to hurt Gwen's either. And I knew she was watching, even though she was trying not to look like she was.

"Thanks," I managed to say, stepping back from him. I gave them all a smile I hoped looked confident, but probably looked more like pathetic. Then I walked over to the edge of the stage, where I found Dane waiting.

"Hey," he said with an easy smile. He was leaning against the stair railing, looking annoyingly calm and confident. "Can you believe this insanity?"

"No," I said as Sarah and her dad began their welcomes and speeches. "I'll just be glad when this is over."

"Stage fright?" he asked.

"A little," I admitted weakly.

"Just pretend you're baking for Say It With Flour," he said. "Nothing else."

I nodded and drew in a shaky breath. It sounded good in theory, but putting it into practice was a different story altogether.

"Did your dad come?" Dane whispered to me as Mayor Chan went on and on about the mall.

"No. He had to open the bakery. But my grandma and brother are here." I scanned the crowd and caught sight of them sitting toward the front. "Is your dad here?"

He shook his head. "My mom's here, though. She's standing over there." He pointed to a pretty woman with blond hair chatting with another mom. "I'm glad she came, especially since my dad had to go on *another* business trip. This time to Chicago. He wants to open another Perk Up there, which means he'll probably want us to move . . . again."

"Oh," I said, reading a flicker of disappointment on his face at the same moment I felt a sharp pang of it. "Will you?"

"Not if I can help it," he said. "I told him I wasn't planning on moving again until college. My mom wants to stay here, too. Between the two of us, we might've finally gotten his attention, so maybe he'll listen this time."

"I hope he does," I said, and I realized how much I truly meant it. Just then, Sarah walked to the edge of the stage and motioned for us to get ready.

Dane looked at me, his eyes serious. "Ali, good luck today. No matter what happens with this contest, I hope we stay friends."

For the first time, I didn't try to decode the look on his face, or search for signs of dishonesty. I didn't want to. Instead, I wanted simply . . . to believe in him.

"Thanks," I said. "Good luck to you, too."

Sarah announced our names into the microphone, and the crowd burst into applause and shouts of encouragement. I followed Dane up the stairs on quaking legs. I took a spot behind one work station and Dane took the other.

"Okay, ladies and gentlemen," Sarah said, "Alicia and Dane

both have identical ingredients in front of them. Flour, butter, sugar, vanilla, baking powder, baking soda, eggs, milk, cocoa powder, cinnamon, and a variety of dried fruits, nuts, and candies. They have to use all of the first ten ingredients and then can use the fruits, nuts, and candies to accessorize. Because cake pops have to chill before they can be decorated, we'll take a two-hour break for lunch and games after the baking is done. Then Dane and Alicia will be back to decorate this afternoon. And finally, a panel of judges will taste test the cake pops and cast anonymous votes to decide the big winner!"

Sarah beamed at her audience, Dane grinned confidently, and I grabbed the edge of the counter, trying not to faint.

A roar went up from the crowd, and chants of "Team Ali" and "Team Dane" broke out all over the park.

"You will have an hour and a half to complete the first half of the bake-off!" She turned to us, clapping her hands. "Good luck to both of you! You may begin!"

The crowd's cheering reached deafening heights as Sarah set a huge timer on the stage. Dane immediately slipped his earbuds on and tuned in to his iPod. I felt a new swell of nerves as I saw the look of casual concentration come over his face. He began tossing ingredients about, barely giving them time to rest in his measuring cups before dumping them helter-skelter into mixing bowls.

I brought my focus back to my own station, wishing I had a way to unplug from reality like Dane did. I examined the ingredients laid out neatly in front of me. The timer was ticking away already, and I had to start. There was only problem. The measuring cups, the mixing bowls, the ingredients — they all looked as alien to me as if I'd never baked a thing in my entire life. I was drawing a complete and total blank.

I looked out at the audience and caught sight of Gwen and Tansy watching expectantly, and Gwen shrugged her shoulders in a "What gives?" gesture. I swallowed as a clammy panic crept over me. I couldn't just stand up here doing nothing while Dane baked and won by default. Then we'd lose Say It With Flour and it really *would* be my fault.

Say It With Flour. I thought about its cheerful yellow walls, the smell of cinnamon and chocolate in the air, the way the seats of the booths squeaked when you sat on them. I thought about my mother baking in that kitchen, using her hands and nothing else.

Suddenly, I knew what I had to do. I took a deep breath, closed my eyes, and reached for my ingredients. I dabbed my finger into a bowl and brought it to my nose. Cocoa. I tried it again with another bowl. There was the cinnamon. And the flour.

I kept my eyes closed and began scooping out ingredients with my hands, just like I had every night for the past week. And as I did, the crowd died away. I heard nothing. I felt nothing, except the silkiness of flour and graininess of sugar filtering through my fingers.

Only when I'd combined all the ingredients into the bowl did I risk opening my eyes. I tentatively dipped a spoon into the batter and tasted it.

It was . . . divine.

Dane and I both worked steadily through the lunch break. While the cakes baked and then cooled, we sifted through the extras of fruits and candies to come up with unique toppings and accessories. While the band put on a concert for everyone in the park, we crushed cookies and berries, swirling and painting with icing. I could hear Dane working beside me, but I kept my eyes on my own pops, not wanting to jinx the rhythm I had going.

Finally, I finished decorating with confidence, knowing I'd made . . . well . . . a masterpiece.

I'd never felt better about anything I'd ever baked.

The final buzzer sounded at four sharp, and Sarah returned to the stage, where a long table had been set up for the judges.

"Welcome back, everyone," Sarah called as the crowd roared. "The judges are about to take their seats. Their names were drawn randomly from Mayor Chan's hat." Applause rose up from the crowd. "Kim Langly, Scott Hicks, Fern Thomson, Jim Mills, and Danielle Newman come on up please."

I watched as five kids took seats at the table and Sarah blindfolded each of them. I recognized their faces from school, but I didn't know any of them well. Sarah placed two cake pops — one of mine, and one of Dane's — in front of each of them. I'd used deep-red candy melts for my cake pop's coating, and then shaped tiny petals around it with icing to make the shape of a rose. Then, I'd dusted the tips of the petals in dark chocolate and gold sugar crystals. Dane had used dark chocolate candy melts for his coating, then molded some of the coating into stiff peaks to make a miniature mountaintop on his pop. He'd used marshmallow fluff, coconut, and gray jelly beans for tiny rocks and snow. My cake pop was beautiful, but I had to admit that Dane's was a work of art, too.

The OCMS band started a drumroll. My stomach tightened with anxiety.

"Ladies and gentlemen," Sarah said, beaming, "let the taste-testing begin!"

The judges carefully took several bites of each pop, drinking water in between. When they were finished eating, they took off their blindfolds to make their votes on slips of paper. One by one, they turned in their votes to Sarah, who tallied them. A heavy silence hung over the park, as if the entire crowd was holding its breath. I couldn't bring myself to look at Abuelita, or even Gwen and Tansy. I couldn't bear the thought of seeing any hint of doubt or nervousness on their faces.

"We have a winner!" Sarah announced happily.

I gripped the counter, my heart exploding. I knew my cake pop tasted good. I knew it had to be the one. It just had to be. . . .

"Dane McGuire!" Sarah spun around and grabbed Dane in a hug that was a little too long, a little too enthusiastic, and altogether too girlfriend-ish. But Dane's ear-to-ear grin said he didn't mind at all.

Jake and the rest of Dane's friends from cross-country whooped and hollered loud congratulations, but the rest of the crowd broke into a mixture of cheers and protests. It was all a vague, distant static in my ears as I robotically moved down the stairs, nodded and smiled politely through dozens of sympathetic handshakes and condolences, and finally found the protective arms of Abuelita Rosa.

"It's all right, *niñita*," she said softly.

"Please just take me home," I whispered, and she nodded, moving me toward the car.

Gwen, Tansy, and Harris followed us, each offering their own versions of pep talks. But in my daze of disappointment, their voices all blurred together. I managed to numbly respond, saying things to make them believe I was okay. But Abuelita knew better.

"She'll call you all *mañana*," she said, tucking me into the car. "Tomorrow."

As she shut my door, my friends' faces were masked in worry. I pulled a smile up from somewhere inside me so they would feel better. That smile was still on my face when I caught sight of Dane jogging toward our car. *His* victory smile was gone, and something that looked like regret seemed to be shining out of his eyes.

I raised my hand to the window, and he brought his hand up in a wave, too. And then I turned away, because the tears I'd been holding in burst out, and the dreams I had of saving our bakery washed away in the flood.

Chapter Twelve

The phone rang the next morning before I'd gotten out of bed. Abuelita stuck her head around my door to let me know it was Gwen. I pulled the covers tighter over my head, pretending to be asleep even though I'd been awake for hours.

"Tell her I'm never leaving my room again," I mumbled with my face buried in my pillow.

"She knew you'd say that." Abuelita whipped the pillow out from under my head. With arms folded, she stood over me looking cross, which I thought was unfair considering how miserable I was. "If you don't come to the phone, she said she's going to come over and drag you out of the house in your pajamas. And if she doesn't, *I* will." Abuelita raised one stern eyebrow. "*¡Levántate! Get up! Arriba ya del caballo, hay que aguantar los reparos.* You're on the horse, so now you must bear it when it rears."

"Argh!" I cried, punching my mattress. "Do you always have to have an answer for everything?"

Abuelita chuckled and shut the door, calling as she walked away, "Of course, *niñita*! What else is old age good for?"

I groaned, then threw back my covers to see the sun shining through my window. The clock read ten A.M. I *never* stayed in bed that long. Reluctantly, I dragged myself out to the phone in the kitchen.

When I picked up, Gwen was ready and waiting.

"Okay, you've exceeded your allotted mope time. Get showered and dressed. Harris and I are taking you to the movies."

I sunk my head onto my arm. That was the last thing I wanted to do today. "Gwen, I'm really not in the mood."

"Which is exactly why we're taking you," Gwen retorted. "I know you feel awful about the bake-off. I do, too. But even if you won, it was a long shot that you were going to change your dad's mind anyway."

"It could've happened," I said, and I still believed it. That's what killed me. I still thought I could have saved Say It With Flour. But now Perk Up would cater Sarah's party. And if anything came of Renata DeLuca's staff being at the bake-off, then Perk Up might even get a shout-out on her show.

And last night, when I told Dad I'd lost the bake-off, I'd seen disappointment cross his face. Maybe he'd been thinking it was a last chance, too. He just hadn't wanted to tell me. And now it was all over for us and Say It With Flour.

"Come on." Gwen's voice was softer now. "You can't obsess over the bake-off forever."

I sighed. "I can if you'll let me."

"Sorry," Gwen said. "Pity parties aren't part of my BFF repertoire."

"Look," I said. "*You* should just go with Harris. Tell him I'm not up for it. This could be your shot with him, and I'm not going to tag along as a third wheel —"

"Ali," Gwen cut me off, her tone suddenly shifting into a clipped tightness. "Here's the deal. This was all Harris's idea. He texted me about it first thing this morning." There was an awkward pause, and then I heard Gwen sigh. "Don't you get it? He wants to go to the movie with *you*, not me. I think he just asked me to come along to be nice."

I shook my head, my pulse jackhammering in my ears. I'd been trying hard to avoid this whole situation, and now here it was, slapping me in the face. "No, that's not true. We're all friends."

"Yeah, and you're totally saying that for my benefit, which is so not helpful." She snorted into the phone. "Listen, if Harris likes you, then I'm over him, period. Or . . . I'll *be* over him in a few nanoseconds. That's the way it has to be."

"He doesn't like me. He can't," I said, but my voice had a certainty I didn't feel. Hadn't I already seen some signs that he did? But I could hear the hurt in Gwen's voice, and I wondered if, or how, our friendship would survive this. Had I just repaired things with Tansy to lose my other BFF?

"I don't know how *you* feel about *him*," Gwen said drily. "I mean, the only guy you ever talk about is Dane. But get ready, because Harris is about to make a move."

"I'm so sorry, Gwen," I whispered.

"Hey, no biggie." Her voice cracked, but then she quickly covered it up by clearing her throat. "I mean, who wouldn't want to get sucked into a Valentine's schmalentine's vortex with Harris?"

I gripped the phone, my heart jerking to a halt. Any other girl would've been ecstatic about Harris, but the butterflies in my stomach were more demented than happy. And I suddenly knew with absolute certainty that I didn't like Harris. Not in that way. And I needed to tell him ASAP, before things between Gwen and me imploded.

"I'll come to the movie," I said. "I'll be ready in an hour."

The movie was a comedy, and I played along, laughing at all the right parts so that Gwen and Harris would think I was feeling better. But it was all an act.

I'd made sure to take an aisle seat so that Gwen and Harris were sitting next to each other, but even so, I could feel Gwen stiff as a board beside me. To make matters worse, the sharp disappointment I felt about the bake-off cut into me over and over. I kept wondering what I'd done wrong. What had the judges tasted in Dane's cake pop that was so much better than mine?

"So did you like it?" Harris asked as we walked out of the darkened theater.

"Oh yeah!" I lied enthusiastically. "I loved it."

He smiled. "What was your favorite part?"

Uh-oh. I hadn't prepared for that question. "Um, well, there were so many good parts. Like when . . . when . . ."

Gwen whirled to face me, her eyes narrowing. "You have no idea what happened in the movie, do you?"

I threw up my hands, blowing hair out of my face. "No! I don't. I'm sorry."

Gwen looked toward the ceiling, shaking her head. "Okay, I need provisions for round two of 'Cheer Up Ali.' Raisinetes are calling."

"I'll come," I said.

"No," she said quickly and a bit forcefully. She shot me a look that said she was doing this on purpose, to give Harris his chance. Then she headed toward the concession stand while I withered inside. "I'll be back."

Desperate, I made a move to follow her anyway, but Harris put his hand on my arm to stop me, and my stomach plunged. Because here it was, the moment alone with Harris that I'd been trying so hard to avoid for the past few weeks. This was my moment to have the "we're just friends" talk with him right now, while Gwen was out of earshot. But before I could muster up the courage to start, he did.

"I'm really sorry about the bake-off, Ali," he said. "I guess you're having a pretty rough weekend, huh?"

I nodded. "You guys should've just come to the movie without me. You would've had more fun."

Harris smiled kindly. "Nah. It's always fun to hang around you. And it's awesome that you're so close to Gwen. She'd be a total wild card if you and your family weren't around. She told me how tough it is not to have her parents around most nights."

"She told you that?" I said, surprise making my voice shift higher. "She never talks about that with anyone except me and Tansy."

"Yeah, it sort of came out of nowhere, but we've been talking a lot lately." Harris blushed and shifted his eyes toward the concession stand, where Gwen was busy arguing with the cashier over the price of Raisinettes. "She's so different from other girls, but in a cool way." A smile spread across his face — a secretive sort of smile I'd never seen on him before.

And suddenly, I knew Gwen had it all wrong, and so did I. Relief flooded through me as I realized who Harris *really* wanted for his valentine.

"Ali, I wanted to ask you something," Harris said, staring at the ground. "Do you think . . ."

"Gwen might be into you?" I finished for him, and grinned when I saw happiness bloom across his face. "That's why you've been hanging around the bakery so much?"

He ducked his head sheepishly. "I thought Gwen might tell you if she liked me. I love your baking, too, but . . . Yeah, I knew I could always find Gwen at the bakery."

Of course. I couldn't believe I hadn't figured it all out before. *That* was what Harris had wanted to talk to me about. He'd wanted to get a read on Gwen, not ask *me* out. It seemed so obvious now — Harris and Gwen using each other as playful punching bags, their *Dragonlore* competitions, Harris being so interested in Gwen's jewelry-making. I could see how perfectly Harris could be the sugar to Gwen's spice.

"So," Harris said now. "Do you think I should go for it? I mean, she's got a pretty high wall of defense. And I don't want her to freak out."

"She won't freak out." I grinned. "Trust me."

Gwen turned toward us, and her eyes were on Harris and Harris alone, disappointment written all over her face. If she thought she was getting over Harris, she was dead wrong.

"Definitely go for it," I whispered to Harris. "I think you two would be great together."

Harris beamed. "Thanks, Ali," he said quietly, right before Gwen came up to us and slugged him on the arm.

"Hey, who wants to play me at *Zombie Invasion* in the arcade?" she asked.

"Not me," I said quickly, jumping at the opening. "I'm going to head home."

"Really?" She frowned, and I could tell she was trying to figure out what had happened while she was gone.

I nodded firmly. "It's pop quiz week in math."

Gwen rolled her eyes. "Some things never change." She looked at Harris. "And I guess you're going, too, then?"

"No way," he said quickly, with a grin. "Bring on the zombies."

"Okay, then," Gwen said, clearly mystified by our behavior. She turned to me. "So could you at least lie and tell me we cheered you up a little it? I'll feel like a failure as a BFF if I didn't."

I hugged her. "You did," I said, figuring the white lie wouldn't hurt anything. I didn't want to be all doom and gloom around them, especially when Gwen was about to get some really great news.

Outside, I hopped on my bike and turned off Hacienda Drive toward Main Street. As I rode, I thought about Gwen and Harris. I was genuinely happy for both of them, and thankful that Harris had never liked me in the first place. I felt about Harris the way I feel about plain vanilla cupcakes. They're sweet and yummy, sure, but they don't have much gusto. I like more *picante* in my baking.

Suddenly, a face flashed across my mind, a face with blond hair and minty eyes. My cheeks heated up unwillingly, taking me by surprise, just like they do when I bite into a Mexican chocolate cupcake laced with cayenne pepper. My favorite.

Chapter Thirteen

When I set foot on campus on Monday morning, something in the air shifted. I'd heard kids chatting and laughing in the hallways, but when they saw me, their voices dipped into whispers.

Tyler and Angie were the first to stop by my locker.

"It's such a bummer about the bake-off," Tyler said.

"Thanks," I mumbled, pasting on my best attempt at an "I'm fine" smile. I must have looked pretty pathetic, though, because Angie grabbed me in a fierce hug, and I didn't even know her that well to begin with.

"It's so unfair," she whispered. "We all tasted your pops, and you should've won. Everyone knows it."

I thanked her, and then started to put my books away, but soon more kids were coming up to me, offering their "sorry's" and "nice try's," too.

"It's okay, really," I said to one person after another. "Dane's an amazing baker. He deserved to win."

I thought I was keeping it together and had my rote response down pat until I passed Dane in the hallway with Jake and Toby. He froze midstep, and Jake and Toby muttered something about getting to class and made the quickest exit I'd ever seen. Once they were gone, Dane opened his mouth to say something, but I beat him to it.

"Congratulations," I said, offering up that smile again. "I'm really happy for you."

I thought my smile could fool him. I was wrong.

"I'm sorry," he said quietly. "I wish things had turned out differently. I wish you'd won."

"You don't have to say that," I mumbled.

"I know," he said. "But I mean it."

I shrugged, biting my lip so he wouldn't catch on to its quivering. "Well, it doesn't matter," I said, making my voice breezy. "My dad's mind was made up anyway. The bakery's closing, and that's that."

I stared at the ground, feeling his eyes searching my face.

"Are you still going to come to Sarah's party on Saturday?" he asked. "It'd be fun if you were there."

"You know, my wardrobe's sadly lacking in pink and red," I said, as if that were the main reason. "I think I'm going to pass."

"That's a bummer," he said. "But, we're okay? I mean, we're still . . . friends?"

"Of course!" I said brightly. I put the smile on again and held it there for proof. "See you in class!" And then I walked away before he could see my face cave in on itself.

I kept my head down, and nearly slammed into Gwen and Tansy.

"Oh, Ali," Tansy said shakily. "We drove by Say It With Flour this morning and saw the sign. It makes me want to cry."

I winced, recalling the forlorn GOING OUT OF BUSINESS sign that Dad had hung in our bakery window. "I know. It's awful."

Gwen patted my shoulder. "How are you holding up?"

I shook my head. "I just saw Dane."

"I figured as much," Gwen said. "You have your Dane face on."

My eyebrows shot up. "I have a Dane face?"

"Sure," Gwen said. "Kind of a tortured, 'I don't know whether to kiss him or punch him' look. You've had that face a lot lately."

I gawked at them. "I have?"

Tansy nodded. "Yes, you have."

"You're the only one who doesn't know you like him." Gwen rolled her eyes. "I even told Harris all about my Ali/Dane, love/hate theory, and he totally agreed. Of course, that was when we *weren't* busy planning our date for Valentine's Day."

Tansy gaped at her. Gwen smiled slyly.

"He asked you out?" I gasped, faking surprise.

She nodded, her face beaming with a very un-Gwen-like sappiness. "But you already knew he was going to, didn't you?"

I shrugged, smiling for real. "Maybe Cupid told me."

"That's amazing!" Tansy shrieked, hugging Gwen.

"Of course, he had to be a total oblivious guy and confuse the heck out of me first . . . and *you*," Gwen said to me. "I'm sorry I got weird about it."

"I'm sorry it got so confusing," I said. "But for the record, I never would've gone out with him anyway."

"Oh, good." She laughed. "I thought I would be okay with you and Harris together, but as it turns out, I'm not that crush-immune."

"Maybe no one is," Tansy said thoughtfully, and I could suddenly feel myself blushing. Tansy could be more insightful than people realized. She snuck a look at me and added, "Cupid might still have some arrows left for you, too."

"Nah," I said, trying to sound nonchalant. "I don't think so."

But when I took my seat next to Dane in world science, my friends' words rung in my ears. My heart started to pound wildly. Maybe it was time to admit to myself that what Gwen had said was true — I *did* like Dane, more than I wanted to admit to myself.

But it didn't matter much now. Whatever chance I'd had with Dane I'd lost along with the bake-off. Because now there was something strung so tight between us, it was impossible to shift back to normal.

Nothing else felt normal the rest of the week. The kids at school were working themselves up into a frenzy about Sarah's birthday party. Valentine's cards, flowers, and candy exploded from everyone's lockers. Even Gwen wore a silly, crush-struck grin when she discovered a *Dragonlore* Valentine in her locker from Harris.

By the time I left school on Friday afternoon, I was sick of Valentine's Day. When I walked into the bakery, I should've been relieved that there wasn't a single paper heart in sight. I should've been relieved that I could lose my stuck-on smile. But I wasn't. The bakery was quiet, still, and sad. Sure, Mrs. Kerny, Mr. Salez, and Mr. Johnson were there in their usual seats. But none of them were talking. They sat glumly, like they were in mourning for a dear, departing friend. This was the new normal, and it was awful.

I set down my bag and mechanically began helping my dad with inventory in the back. We had to get a count of everything in the shop before we could sell anything. I was in the middle of tallying canisters of flour in the back pantry when a loud shout from the front of the shop nearly made me fall off my step ladder.

"Ali!" There it was again.

I froze. I knew that voice. I jumped off the ladder and hurried through the swinging door.

And sure enough, there was an out-of-breath Dane, his face flushed with excitement.

"Ali," he said, gulping air. "I ran over here from school. I have to tell you something. You're not going to believe it."

"Okay," I said uncertainly.

Dane grinned. "Perk Up's not going to cater Sarah's party. I backed out of the job."

My eyes widened. "What are you talking about?"

"Sarah rigged the bake-off," he said. "She didn't tally the votes correctly after the taste test. Your cake pops actually got the most votes, but she lied and announced me as the winner."

I shook my head, trying to make sense of it all. "But why would she do that?"

"She wanted me to win the bake-off," he said. "She was the one who put the black food coloring in your pops at the jewelry show, too! She was hoping if you looked like a horrible baker, she could drop you from the bake-off altogether and just hire me. But her dad wouldn't let her."

I collapsed into the nearest booth, stunned. "But . . . how did you even find out about all of this?"

Dane sat down across from me. "I overheard some of the kids who were the judges saying that they'd voted for you and you should've won. It bothered me all week, so finally today, I tracked down all the judges and asked them how they voted. We tallied the votes again, and your cake pops had the most." He paused, and I tried to let this reality sink in. "So I asked Sarah about it," Dane went on, drumming his long fingers on the tabletop. "At first she acted like she had no idea what I was talking about, but then when the judges called her on it, she broke down and confessed everything."

"That is complete craziness," I said. "I don't get it. I've never done anything to Sarah! Why would she have it out for me?"

Dane's cheeks blazed red, and a look of embarrassment crossed his face. "Well, it turns out . . ." He laughed a little. "She has, or had, a crush on me. She thought if she made sure I won the bake-off and catered her party, she could get me to like her, too. And you know Sarah. She's used to getting what she wants."

"Oh." I dropped my eyes to the table, a leaden weight sinking my stomach. "I guess that makes sense." I gulped, knowing I had to ask the next question, but not sure I wanted to hear the answer. "So . . . do you? Like her, I mean?"

Dane stared at me for a second, and then burst out laughing. "Of course not! Why would I ever go for a girl like that?"

I smiled, feeling a bubbly hope rising again. "I don't know. She's so pretty and popular. I thought maybe . . ."

He leaned toward me, serious now. "Real is better than popular any day."

He held my eyes until I dropped mine, flustered. All week we'd been tiptoeing around each other, politely chatting in class, nodding in the hallways. But I'd missed the easy way we'd fallen into talking before the bake-off ever happened. I even missed our fights. Now, it was like the old Dane was back, and I was thrilled to see him again.

He stood up. "So we'd better get to work. I hope your dad hasn't gotten rid of any baking equipment yet."

"He hasn't," I said. "Why?"

He took my hands and pulled me up out of the booth. "Because, since *I'm* not catering Sarah's party tomorrow, *you* are."

I adamantly shook my head. "No way! That's not possible! She invited the entire school. At two cake pops per person, I'd have to make . . ." I paused, doing the numbers in my head.

"Five hundred," Dane finished for me. "You have to make five hundred cake pops by ten o'clock tomorrow morning, and I'm going to help you." He grinned devilishly. "So why are you standing around? The cake pops aren't going to bake themselves!"

I snapped out of my haze of disbelief, smiled at Dane, and then ran into the kitchen, a thrilling giddiness coming over me.

"Dad," I yelled, laughing. "Fire up the oven. We're back in business."

The next morning, I stepped out of the bakery truck into the world's biggest Valentine. Even the drive leading up to Chan Manor was covered in pink gravel and rose petals. Two massive tents with pale pink drapes bordered the Olympic-size swimming pool, clusters of pink balloons bursting up from their corners. Two-foot centerpieces of blushing roses sat at every table, and heart confetti was strewn across every pale pink tablecloth. A lot of kids from school were already there, swimming in the pool and taking turns riding Sarah's horse. (Yes, Mayor Chan had given Sarah an actual live horse for her birthday. Yeesh.) To keep in the spirit of the party, and to keep on Sarah's good side, everyone was wearing red and pink clothes or bathing suits.

"Well, at least I made the cake pops the right color," I said. I slid a box holding a bouquet of fifty red and pink heart-shaped cake pops out of the back of the truck. They were an all-new recipe — black forest ganache with the teeniest hint of chili powder for a little kick. I'd used an edible ink pen to write "We ♥ Sarah" on each one (even though I'd *wanted* to write quite the opposite). But they looked fantastic, if I did say so myself.

"This is not a birthday party," Gwen said, balancing another box of pops in her arms. "This is Cupid overload."

"It's not so bad, Gwen. You do look pretty in pink," Harris said, making her blush with such uncharacteristic sweetness that the rest of us couldn't help staring.

I leaned my head on Gwen's shoulder. "I couldn't have done it without you." Then I turned to Dane, Harris, Tansy, and my dad, who were each holding boxes of pops. "I couldn't have done this without any of you."

Last night, all of us had worked in the bakery until three in the morning to make the five hundred cake pops for the party. Even Abuelita Rosa and Roberto had helped for awhile, until Roberto fell asleep with his cheek in a puddle of batter. I knew my friends were all exhausted today, but they'd hung in there for me and my dad. I was exhausted, but filled with hope. If I could pull this off, maybe, just maybe, we could still save the bakery.

"Well," I said, taking a deep breath. "Let's get these set up on the tables."

We carefully placed one pink vase on each table with a bouquet of pops nestled inside. When everything was ready, Sarah came over to see. I wanted to stomp on her foot — and from Gwen's and Tansy's expressions, they looked close to doing it themselves — but we all remained aloof and civilized. Sarah scrutinized every bouquet with shrewd eyes, and then cautiously took one of the pops and walked toward a microphone that had been set up on the lawn. Her father stood nearby, watching.

"What is she doing?" Tansy whispered.

"I have no idea," I said, suddenly worrying that this could go very badly.

"If I could have everyone's attention for just a moment," Sarah said into the microphone. "I just wanted to say a big thank-you to Alicia for making these cake pops on such short notice." She bit into her cake pop.

I held my breath as she chewed, and finally, after what felt like an eternity, she nodded.

"Mmmm . . . they're perfect." She smiled brilliantly, clapping in my direction. "Thanks, Ali." She started to walk away from the mike, but Mayor Chan cleared his throat loudly. Sarah froze, blushing madly.

I stared in disbelief. It was the first time I'd ever seen Sarah lose her cool composure. She returned to the mike, stuttering her words out.

"Um, I also wanted to apologize for the misunderstanding at the bake-off," she added hurriedly. "Alicia was, of course, the true winner. I still don't know how on earth I managed to miscount the votes, but I guess I need to pay more attention in math from now on!" She laughed lightly, and a few kids in the pool area joined in politely. But most of them were eyeing her suspiciously. Word of her meddling and tricks had spread throughout the school — and even Lissie and Jane were angry at her for turning their teeth black. I realized Sarah had finally lost some of her influence. It would be a nice change of pace at OCMS.

Mayor Chan gave a slight nod of approval, and Sarah finished with, "Enjoy the pool and the pops!"

She tossed her empty cake-pop stick in the trash, brushed the crumbs daintily from her fingers, then walked back to us.

"I hope you all enjoy the party." She looked at each of us in turn, dwelling on Dane's face a teensy bit longer than the rest. Then she turned back to me. "My dad has your check ready for you. He added in a little bit extra, since you were able to take the job on such short notice. See you later!"

She started prancing across the lawn in her pink chiffon dress, but Mayor Chan stopped her, and to Sarah's obvious mortification, brought her right back to me. One stern glance from him, and Sarah's composure wilted.

"Um, Ali, there is one other thing I forgot to tell you," she mumbled, staring at the ground. "To make up for everything that happened, I'm supposed to . . . I mean, I have to . . ."

"She'd like to volunteer to help out at the bakery," Mayor Chan finished, since Sarah was clearly at a loss for words. "Every Saturday for the next month. I'm sure you could find a good job for her."

I smiled. Oh, this was too good to be true. "Sure," I said cheerfully. "We could always use extra help in the kitchen with dishes and cleanup."

"That sounds perfect," Mayor Chan said, patting Sarah on the shoulder. "She looks forward to it. Don't you, sweetie?"

"Sure, Dad," Sarah muttered.

"Great!" I said. "So I'll see you next Saturday at six A.M., then."

"Six!" Sarah practically shrieked, and Gwen snorted a laugh into her elbow.

I nodded. "We always open bright and early!"

"She'll be there," Mayor Chan said, then lead Sarah away as she hissed protests under her breath and the rest of us broke into fits of giggles.

"Sweet justice at last," I said. "I wonder if I can put her on bathroom detail?"

"Be nice, Ali," Tansy mock-scolded.

"But not too nice," Gwen said. "Seeing Sarah eat humble pie just made this whole pinkified party worthwhile."

"Anybody want to dive into the pool?" Tansy asked.

"Are you kidding me?" I laughed. "I wouldn't pass up a chance to swim at Chan Manor. Let's go."

Within ten minutes, we had changed into our swimwear (I

was a little shy wearing my new red bathing suit in front of Dane, but after a while I relaxed). Tansy, Gwen, Harris, Dane, and I splashed and swam in the pool. My dad had gone inside to settle up the invoice with Mayor Chan. It was a cloudless California day, and the water was bathtub warm. We swam for over an hour, but then I looked over to see my dad beckoning me over to the side.

"Dad?" I swam over to him, watching his pale face with concern. "What's wrong?"

"Nothing's wrong. I think I'm just in shock." He smiled at me. "Mayor Chan just told me that he wants us to make a thousand cake pops for the grand opening of the mall next month. And apparently, some cooking-show woman named Renee Denada wants to interview you on her show. She called Mayor Chan this morning to get more information about Sarah's party pops. She's doing a segment on young entrepreneurs."

I almost fell backward and underwater.

"Do you mean Renata DeLuca?" I gasped. "But how did she find out about me?"

"Her show called Perk Up to interview me after the bake-off," Dane said, swimming up beside me. "But then I told them that *you* were actually the winner, and they needed to talk to you."

"She wants to talk to me about my baking," I whispered, letting it sink in. Then I whooped and yelled, "Renata DeLuca wants to talk to me!"

My dad beamed. "Alicia, with the cake pops from today's order and the mall opening," he said, "we'll have enough revenue to stay open through the spring. And then we can see what happens from there."

Without thinking, I jumped out of the pool and hugged my dad, not caring one bit that I was getting his pants and shirt soaking wet. He laughed, so I figured he didn't care, either.

"That's amazing, Dad," I said, kissing his cheek. "We'll keep it open. I know we will! I thought of this great new idea, just this morning. I can open a baked goods delivery service. I can call it Bake 'n' Bike. I can deliver cake pops and pastries to people on my bike around town, and then maybe we can branch out even more. . . ."

My dad held up his hands, chuckling. "Slow down, slow down. We can talk about all this later. Right now, I'm going to the bakery to take down that awful 'Going Out of Business' sign. You enjoy your time with your friends, and I'll come back to pick you up later." He gave me one last hug, and then walked away just as Gwen and Tansy erupted in wild screams, splashing through the water to pull me back into the pool and drown me in hugs.

"Perk Up's in serious trouble now," Dane said with a grin.

"So I guess this means we're guaranteed all-you-can-eat pops for life," Gwen said.

"I've already decided I'm going to have my birthday party *at* Say It With Flour," Tansy said.

"And Gwen and I want to have a twenty-four-hour *Dragonlore* marathon." Harris grinned at me. "Now we have the perfect place."

"But, it'll cost you," I teased. "Can't give away services for free, you know."

They all blinked at me, and when they realized I was joking, they sent a tidal wave of splashes in my direction. I threw my head back, laughing, and feeling the heavy load of worries I'd carried with me for the last month flying away. The bakery was ours again, and it would stay that way. I was sure of it. Someday, it would be mine, and maybe Roberto's, too. Just the way Mom had wanted it.

We swam for a while longer and then we wrapped up in towels to sit around the outdoor fire pit. When it was time for everyone to sing to Sarah and eat their cake pops, Gwen, Tansy, and Harris stood up to head toward the tents.

"Are you coming?" Gwen asked me.

I shook my head. "Nah. I think I'll hang out here. After the last two weeks, I'm a little cake-popped out."

"I'll stay here and make sure she keeps out of trouble," Dane said to them.

"Okay," Gwen said, giving me a knowing grin that I could've killed her for. "You two have fun."

I ducked my head, embarrassed. But when I braved a glimpse at Dane, he had a curious smile on his face, like he'd just had a question answered for him.

I took a deep breath, my heart racing. "You know, I never got a chance to say thank you."

His brow crinkled. "For what?"

"For all your help last night, and for Renata DeLuca, and . . ." I waved my hands toward the party tent. "For this. I know you didn't have to turn down Sarah's party," I said. "You still could've catered it."

His brow furrowed. "No. It wouldn't have been right. I tasted your cake pop. It was way better than mine. You should've won the bake-off, and you deserved to cater the party."

"Was your dad mad that you backed out?"

Dane shrugged. "Sure, because he's always looking at the bottom line. But he'll get over it. Your Bake 'n' Bike idea will give him plenty more to worry about. I wish I'd thought of that great one." He gave my shoulder a nudge.

"Don't even think of stealing it!" I mock-glared.

"Hey, I know better than to mess with a shrewd businesswoman like you. Besides, I like that you're keeping Perk Up on its toes. Maybe my dad will let us stay here forever, just to keep an eye on you." He smiled. "He and my mom already agreed that we could stay here longer, so maybe he's coming around a little."

"That's great!" I said. The thought of Dane staying in Oak Canyon made me feel even happier. But then another sobering thought struck me. "Are you sure you didn't back out of Sarah's party because you felt sorry for me?" I asked quietly. "For the bakery?"

"I didn't feel sorry for you or for your store. When I first saw Say It With Flour, I actually felt a little jealous. Perk Up is just a moneymaker to my dad. Even though I love the baking part of it, sometimes I hate what Perk Up does to my dad, and our family." He stared at the ground for a long time, but when he looked up, there was a shyness on his face I'd never seen before. "So I guess I did want to help you save the bakery," he said. "It's a special place. It's part of who you are." He leaned toward me. "And I like that, because I like you."

"You do?" I whispered, not sure I could let myself believe it.

But then he kissed me.

And I believed him.

The butterflies in my stomach this time were dizzying and magic. I realized Dane had surprised me yet again. Maybe that's why I'd started off disliking him. Because I'd never liked surprises.

But as our lips met in another sweet, soft kiss by the crackling fire, I wondered if I was changing. Surprises still made my stomach flip uneasily. They made my heart race, my hands sweat, my head spin. But now I knew that surprises were also one of the most delicious parts of life. And just like cake pops, I wanted to enjoy them down to the very last bite.

Ali's Recipes

Cake pops are fun to make, and even more fun to eat!
You can give some of Ali's recipes a try, or invent
some of your own. Before you get started,
you'll need some basic cake pop necessities:

- Several packs of cake pop sticks (can be purchased at craft stores or some grocery stores)

- Several 1-pound bags of candy melts (in any colors or flavors you'd like)

- 2–3 Styrofoam blocks to stick your cake pops in while they're setting (can be purchased at craft stores)

- 1 small but deep microwaveable plastic bowl for coating your cake pops

- Sprinkles or mini chocolate chips if you want to decorate your pops

- If you want to mold your cake pops into fun shapes, you'll need at least one miniature cookie cutter (Hearts, butterflies, and flowers — your pick!). Cookie cutters should be about 1½ inches in size.

- Ask a parent or adult to help out with ovens and stove tops. Candy melts can get extremely hot, so be extra careful not to burn yourself. Always use adult supervision when baking, working with hot ingredients, or using ovens or stoves.

- If you need cake pop advice from a real expert, take a look at the book *Cake Pops: Tips, Tricks, and Recipes for More Than 40 Irresistible Mini Treats* by Bakerella. Often acknowledged as the inventor of cake pops, Bakerella has lots of fun, creative ideas for decorating the treats. Plus, there are color photos of tons of fabulous cake pops in the book to use for inspiration.

Pops from a Box

(the easiest recipe for the Cake Pop Newbie)

1 boxed cake mix, any flavor you like
1 16-oz container of premade icing, any flavor as long it's a smooth texture
1 one-pound bag of candy melts, any flavor or color you'd like

Bake the cake in a greased 9x13 pan, according to the instructions on the box. Let the cake cool completely. Once it has cooled, cut the cake into eight sections. Lift out one section at a time. With your hands, crumble each section of the cake into one large mixing bowl. Break up any large chunks with your hands until you've crumbled the entire cake into the bowl, and all of the crumbs are small and about the same size.

Mix ¾ of the canned icing into the bowl with the cake. Use your hands or a large spoon to knead the cake/icing mix until it's well blended. Then, roll the cake pop batter into small balls about 1¼ inches wide. Cover the balls with plastic wrap and chill in the freezer for about 15 minutes.

While the cake balls are chilling, make your candy coating (this should only take 2–3 minutes, so wait until your cake balls are nearly ready to be taken out of the freezer). Melt about ¼ pound of candy melts according to the instructions on the package. If you're using a microwave, heat the melts in a small microwave-safe plastic bowl for twenty seconds at a time, stopping to stir them every twenty seconds. Stop heating as soon as the candy has melted. If you overheat the melts, they will get lumpy, thick, and unusable. When you stir the melted candy, it should run easily off your spoon. If it doesn't, add ½–1 teaspoon of shortening to the bowl to thin the coating. If the coating is too thick, your pops might break off into the bowl when you're trying to coat them.

Once your cake balls are chilled and your coating is melted, you're ready to dip and decorate. Have your cake pop sticks and your Styrofoam blocks handy. Remove just a few cake balls from your freezer at a time, so they don't get too warm. Dip the tip of a cake pop stick into the bowl of melted coating, coating about ¼ inch of the tip. Insert the coated stick about ¼ inch into a cake ball. Then, once the cake ball is stuck on the stick, dip the entire ball into the coating in one swift movement. Try not to roll the pop or dip it for too long, or the ball might fall off or break into the coating bowl. Lift the pop out of the bowl, and carefully turn the pop, tapping the stick with your finger very gently to remove any extra coating. If you want to decorate your pop, now is the time to dip it into a smaller bowl of candy sprinkles or mini chocolate chips. Then stick the cake pop into the Styrofoam block to set. Repeat this process until all of the cake pops are done (you will need to melt more candy melts for coating as you go). Let the coating dry completely. Then pass out pops to friends and family and enjoy every bite!

You can also make similar pops with premade cheesecake. All you have to do is scoop cheesecake into balls (without using the crust portion). Chill the cheesecake balls in the freezer for 15 minutes, then remove, coat, and decorate just like you did with the cake balls.

You will most likely use 1–2 pounds of candy melts for coating for this recipe and for all of the recipes that follow. Each recipe yields between 50–60 cake pops.

A word of encouragement: Don't worry if your first few cake pops don't look too glamorous. It may take a little practice to get the coating on just right. The trick is to keep the coating thin, so you can dip the pops in and out quickly. Have fun, and remember, even if the first few look funny, they'll still taste delish!

Red Velvet Mocha Fudge Pops
(for the Cake Pop Up-and-Comer)

For the cake:
> 2½ cups flour
> 1 tsp baking soda
> 1 tsp cocoa powder
> 1 tsp cinnamon
> 1½ cups sugar
> 1½ cup vegetable oil
> 2 eggs
> 1 tsp vanilla
> 1 one-ounce bottle red food coloring
> 1 tsp vinegar
> 1 cup buttermilk

Preheat oven to 350°. In a medium bowl, mix all of your dry ingredients. In a smaller bowl, mix the oil, eggs, vanilla, food coloring, and vinegar. In a large bowl, mix all these ingredients together, adding small portions of the dry and wet ingredients at a time until completely blended. Finally, add in the buttermilk and blend. Pour the batter into a 9x13 greased pan and bake for 35–45 minutes until a toothpick inserted into the middle comes out clean.

For the mocha fudge frosting:
> ¾ cup cocoa
> 1 stick butter, softened
> 1 tsp vanilla
> ½ tsp salt
> 2 tbsp fresh cold decaffeinated coffee (not instant)
> 2 cups powdered sugar

In a medium bowl, blend all of the ingredients together with a handheld mixer.

For the cake pops:
Follow the instructions for making basic Pops from a Box, but use your crumbled red velvet cake and 1½ cups of your mocha frosting instead. Chill your cake balls. Choose a fun color or flavor for your candy melt coating (chocolate candy melts are perfect for this!). Prepare your coating using about ¼ pound of candy melts at a time, then dip and decorate.

Strawberries and Cream Pops

(for the Cake Pop Adventurer)

For the cake:

    2¾ cup flour

    2½ tsp baking powder

    2 cups granulated sugar

    1 three-ounce package of strawberry Jell-O

    1 cup butter, softened

    4 eggs

    1 cup milk

    2 tsp vanilla

    ½ cup strawberries, pureed

Preheat oven to 350°. In a medium bowl, mix flour and baking powder together. In a large bowl, mix sugar, Jell-O, and butter with a handheld mixer. Add eggs one at a time, mixing as you do. Add the flour and baking powder into the sugar mixture and beat as you add in the milk. Finally, stir in vanilla and pureed strawberries. Pour into 9x13 greased pan and bake for 40–50 minutes, until toothpick inserted into the middle comes out clean.

For the frosting:

    ½ cup butter, softened

    1 eight-ounce pack of cream cheese

    4 cups powdered sugar

    2 tsp vanilla

Mix all the ingredients together with handheld mixer.

For the cake pops:

Follow the instructions for making basic Pops from a Box, but use your crumbled strawberry cake and 1½ cups of your cream cheese frosting instead. Chill your cake balls. Choose a fun color or flavor for your candy melt coating (white chocolate candy melts are yummy with this!). Prepare your coating using about ¼ pound of candy melts at a time. Then dip cake pops and decorate.

Black Forest Heart Pops

(the most challenging recipe for the Cake Pop Goddess)

For the cake:

    ¾ cup cocoa powder

    2 cups sugar

    1¾ cups flour

    1½ tsp. baking soda

    1½ tsp. baking powder

    1 tsp. salt

    1–4 tsp. chili powder (optional)

    1 cup milk

    2 eggs

    2 tsp. vanilla

    ½ cup vegetable oil

    1 cup boiling water (added at the very last)

Preheat your oven to 350°. In a large bowl, mix all of your dry ingredients. Then, add the milk, eggs, vanilla, and vegetable oil, and blend with a handheld mixer. Add the boiling water and mix. Pour the batter into a 9x13 greased pan and bake 35–40 minutes, until a toothpick inserted into the middle of the cake comes out clean.

For the ganache frosting:

    12 oz chopped semisweet baking chocolate

    1 cup heavy cream

    1 can pitted sweet cherries, drained and chopped

Put chopped chocolate into a medium bowl. Boil cream in a sauce-pan. Pour the cream over the chocolate and mix until well blended. Wait to add the cherries into your crumbled cake mixture with the icing (see next page).

For the cake pops:

Follow the instructions for making basic Pops from a Box, but use your crumbled chocolate cake and ¾ cup of your ganache frosting instead. Add the chopped cherries into the crumbled cake, too. Mix it all together with your hands and roll it into balls. To make the pops into heart shapes, allow the cake balls to chill in the freezer for 15 minutes. Then remove them. One by one, press the balls into a mini heart-shaped cookie cutter. Gently push them out of the cookie cutter. Place them back in the freezer for a few minutes to re-chill. Choose a fun color or flavor for your candy melt coating. Prepare your coating using about ¼ pound of candy melts at a time. Then dip the cake pops and decorate.

Don't miss this other delicious read by Suzanne Nelson!

"One last treat before you go," she said, setting down a plate of pastel pink, green, and yellow sandwich-shaped cookies. They were so cute and colorful, with a delicious-looking icing center.

"These are macarons." Madame Leroux placed one in my palm.

"You share the first one . . . like this." She showed me how to carefully twist it apart.

"Cheers," I said, my voice lilting nervously as the boy and I clinked our halves together before eating them. The pink macaron was spongy and crunchy all at once, with the creamy center melting on my tongue in hints of raspberry and vanilla. It was perfect.

"There." Madame Leroux clasped both our hands in satisfaction.

"Two halves connect two people, eh?" She winked.

Shakily, I stood up and walked with the boy to the door.

"Sweet dreams for St. Valentine's," Madame Leroux called to us before she closed the door, leaving us standing outside under a bright, star-sprinkled sky.

My heart galloped as his eyes turned to mine. "That was fun," I said, to break the silence. "I'm lucky I found this place."

"I am, too." His voice was so soft, I wasn't sure I'd heard him right. "You know," he continued, "I didn't want to come here tonight."

"Really?" I asked in surprise. "Why? Who doesn't want to eat yummy pastries?"

He laughed. "The food wasn't the problem. I was standing in for a kid who backed out of an assignment at the last minute."

He frowned. "I wanted to ditch the whole thing to spend the night sketching, but I didn't have the guts. I guess I'm sort of . . . too responsible for my own good." He sighed. A sweet, bashful smile spread across his face, making him look even cuter. "Anyway, what I'm trying to say is . . . tonight was totally worth it."

I nodded. "Yeah, the food was amazing."

He shook his head. "The food's not what made it worth it," he said quietly. My heart trilled as he stepped closer to me. "I'd like to see you again," he said.

"I'm sure you will," I blurted, sounding as nervous as I felt. " 'Cause it's such a small town and . . . and . . ." My voice died. I couldn't breathe, let alone think straight. "I mean, I'd like that."

He stepped closer.

"So how does the fairy tale go?" he whispered, leaning toward me. "The Frog Princess only becomes human again after . . ."

A kiss, I thought deliriously as I closed my eyes. I held my breath, waiting for his soft lips to brush mine. *My first kiss . . .*

"*Espera aí!* Hold it right there!" a stern voice bellowed in my ear, and I jumped as a hand clamped down on my shoulder.

My dad glared down at me. "What do you think you're doing?"

"Dad, I —"

"It's after midnight! I spent the last hour driving around town looking for you. I was about to call the police." He latched on to my arm, firmly tugging me down the sidewalk toward where his car was parked at the curb. He threw open the door of the car and growled, "Get in . . . now!"

"But, Dad . . ." I glanced back toward the awning of Swoonful of Sugar, where the potential boy of my dreams was standing in a state of confusion.

Find more reads
you will love . . .

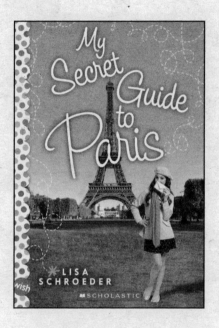

Nora loves everything about Paris, from the Eiffel Tower to chocolat chaud. She's never actually been there — she's only visited through her Grandma Sylvia's stories. So when Nora finds letters and a Paris treasure map among her Grandma Sylvia's things, she dares to dream again . . .

11 Birthdays

WENDY MASS

SCHOLASTIC

wish

It's Amanda's 11th birthday and she is super excited. But everything goes wrong. She and her best friend, Leo, with whom she's shared every birthday, have a fight. When Amanda turns in for the night, glad to have her birthday behind her, she wakes up happy for a new day. Or is it? Her birthday seems to be repeating itself. What is going on? And how can she fix it?

sit,
stay,
love

Girl meets dog.
Girl meets cute boy.
Drama ensues. . .

j.j. howard

📖 SCHOLASTIC

wish

When a cute pug named Potato is brought in to the shelter where Cecilia Murray volunteers, she knows he is the dog she's been waiting for. There's just one problem: Eric Chung — a popular, arrogant boy from school — adopts Potato first. What's worse, he hopes to train the little tater to become a show-dog superstar. So Cecilia sets out to sabotage Eric's plans . . .

How to spot a  book

EYE-CATCHING SPINES!

FUN & FRIENDSHIP INSIDE!

IRRESISTIBLE STORIES!

PLUS, FIRST CRUSHES!